FAMILY SECRET
MEMORIES

ASEMANA
BOOKS

FAMILY SECRET
MEMORIES

Mohammad Qassemzadeh

Translated from the Persian

by Mahshad Abdoli

ASEMANA
BOOKS

Toronto, Canada

FIRST EDITION

The initial draft of this translation was prepared by Mahshad Abdoli. AI tools were used to assist with proofreading, after which the translation was thoroughly reviewed and finalized by her to ensure accuracy, cultural nuance, and fidelity to the original text.

Published by ASEMANA BOOKS

ISBN: 9781997503033

Book Design: Asemana Books

Cover Art: Asemana Books

To find out more about our authors and books visit: www.asemanabooks.ca

ASEMANA
BOOKS

Contents

Chapter 1

Incidents always happen when nobody expects them. Well, if they were already known, they wouldn't be called incidents. However, for me, incidents aren't all that unexpected. That's because I always sense, in advance, that a new disaster is about to happen—thanks to my animal instinct. I actually owe my life to it. I always sniff around like a dog. Well, I've gotten used to it. When the time comes, I am always waiting for the incident to strike, like a pile of rubble about to fall on my head. That's why I'm always preoccupied, trying to use every thought I have to figure it out before it happens. As soon as I get closer to sensing it—or even guessing it—my heart starts pounding. Then, I sit like a hen about to lay an egg. But disasters don't just pass—they crush you, don't they? They say hens feel relieved after laying an egg, but for me, my problems begin the moment I have to struggle with the disaster that strikes me, fighting hard to solve the chaos it brings.

My instinct works well, but if my mind fails me or doesn't help in time, I still manage to escape incidents with my animal instinct. After all, one incident is always followed by another. When the *Week of Happiness,*

Week of Mourning or *Silence Fasting* is about to start, I brace myself for an unfortunate event.

I remember nothing from my childhood except being beaten—beaten by my father, mother, sister, and worst of all, my teachers. Other than that, the only thing I haven't forgotten is our home address. We lived in Star Alley, 164 East Street. Even though we moved away years ago, I still remember the alley's name and the street number. Maybe because my birth certificate number is 164, and my mother and sister used to tell me stories about stars.

I don't handle grief well at all, but the first event that truly saddened and worried me was my father's death. It was before this incident that I first discovered the power of my animal instinct. A week before the celebration of *Happiness Week*, my heart began to race. I couldn't get out of bed in the morning. My mother thought I was sick. She sat beside me, insisting that I move to the living room. I dragged myself out of bed with difficulty and reached the sofa in front of the door, but I couldn't sit down. I lay down again. My mother urged me to see a doctor, but I knew there was nothing physically wrong with me. Still, I couldn't understand what was happening to me.

I was getting worse day by day. Of course, I felt no pain. Even my heartbeat had returned to normal. The only thing I felt was a flutter in my stomach, like butterflies, and the egg was pressing—about to fall—but it never did.

Happiness Week began, but I hadn't recovered at all. By then, I had already realized that instead of pain, an unknown sensation had awakened in my body. When I told my mother, she bit her lip. She must have thought I was going crazy. Two days before the end of *Happiness Week*, I told her, "Something unfortunate is going to happen."

She laughed and said, "Oh great! A fortune teller is all we needed in this ill-mannered family."

Despite her sarcasm, I didn't change my mind. Although I had stayed home for the entire week, for some reason, I was convinced that the unfortunate incident would take place outside.

That incident happened exactly 21 years ago, and it was the worst I could have ever imagined. My father passed away. But in a way, it was a mercy that he died in the early morning of the last day of *Happiness Week*. As his heart stopped beating, I suddenly felt better. It was as if I had been waiting for him to die.

No matter how difficult it was, we kept his body at home for a day. It was a day of joy and celebration, and no one dared to show sadness. That day, I went to the pharmacy twice to buy a special powder to prevent the corpse from smelling due to the heat. Although I was mourning my father's death, I laughed loudly in the alley and on the street, trying to dispel any doubts or suspicions from the people and the police. But officers are never fooled by such laughter. The next day, with the help of acquaintances and friends, we took my father's body to the public cemetery. The private cemetery for authors and journalists had long been closed, so people were forced to bury their dead in unmarked graves, indistinguishable from one another. After we buried him, the police officers approached me, my mother, and my sister and bluntly stated that they would consider my father's death as an obstruction and disruption of *Happiness Week*.

***

My father's body had barely been buried when my mother started recalling her memories of him. But whenever those memories didn't serve her well, she conveniently cut out the important details in her favor. She was a master censor. Yet, I knew exactly what she was omitting and why—because my father had already told me everything in detail over the years, without her knowledge. When he had no one else to talk to, he would sit next to me and share as much as he could about my mother—the things I was supposed to ignore, but when I had no way out, I had to pretend I was asleep. At first, he believed I was really sleeping, but later, he realized I was faking it. So he outsmarted me. When I shut my eyes, he didn't stop talking—he kept going. That's why I didn't believe everything my mother said after his death, and I interrupted her constantly. Then, she lost her temper and threw whatever was within her reach at me. I had learned how to protect myself. I either ran away before she could attack, or I made sure to grab any dangerous object near her before she started talking. Thanks to this trick, I managed to survive the things she viciously threw to hurt me.

When I was a child, my father seemed like a towering figure—a giant. But as I grew taller year by year, he seemed to shrink. In the last years of his life, he had become so short that he barely reached my neck. The shrinking continued until he died. And then, the moment he passed away, he grew tall again—returning to the height he once was.

My parents met during World War II, but not on the battlefield. They met while eating ice cream. My father told me they had both been standing in front of an ice cream shop, waiting for the server to hand them their orders. The server had given my mother a metal container full of ice cream first, and she had offered it to my father. He hadn't accepted it, but he had smiled—knowingly, meaningfully. He had shown me a photograph taken in the early days of their acquaintance. His face had been round and full, radiating energy. His cheeks were flushed red, and his large eyes sparkled with happiness. My mother, on the other hand, had a thin face in the photo. Yet despite her bony features, she didn't look sad or frail. On the contrary, her gray, heavy-lidded eyes reflected an indescribable joy at having met my father. Their only similarity back then was that they were both tall—before my father started shrinking. Eventually, he became so short that his head barely reached my mother's chest.

However, it was crystal clear from the beginning that they did not get along. My father said, "Even the meetings were arranged by your mother. She never met me halfway or accepted what I said."

One day, he told me, "I worked in the north of the city. Your mother scheduled our meetings in the city center, exactly half an hour after I finished work. I had to rush to get there, while she always arrived earlier. By the time I arrived, my heart was pounding. I would just sit down on a chair, struggling to catch my breath. And from that moment on, she was the absolute ruler of the meeting."

At first, he thought my mother insisted on choosing the meeting place to maintain appearances and keep a low profile. But when he noticed that one of her countless relatives conveniently showed up at every meeting, he realized he had been outmaneuvered. Unlike my father, who had no companion, my mother always surrounded herself with others, leaving him no choice but to go wherever she had preselected. After a few meetings, he got used to the presence of her friends—friends who vanished the moment he gave in, never to be seen again, at least not until the day he passed away.

In the final months of the war, she suddenly accused him of spilling the beans. He was bewildered. "When and where did I make a mistake?" he asked. "I never meant to do anything wrong." But my mother revealed, quite clearly, exactly where and when he had slipped up.

According to the story my father told, exactly 75 days before the war ended, he had fled to my mother's paternal uncle's villa in the countryside, north of the city, to escape the soldiers' invasion. Upon his arrival, he was stunned. My mother's uncle—who always described himself as extremely devoted to conventions—handed her the keys and allowed her to spend several days there with a strange man. My father recounted, "Well, your mother stayed with me only for the last three days of that week, but I swear on my father's innocent soul, I didn't do anything at all."

Yet, my mother later confronted him, claiming he was drunk. He always remembered that conversation, even in the last days of his life.

Father: "Cut the crap. I didn't do anything."
Mother: "Oh, but you were drunk. Do you remember what you said that night?"
Father: "Yes, we were discussing the conditions of the planets in the sky."
Mother: "Really? Were you talking about the planets when you were about to throw yourself naked into the river from the villa's rooftop?"

Father: "Was I going to throw myself?"

Mother: "See? You were so drunk you don't remember anything. Tell me, what were you going to do with my uncle's gun?"

Father: "I didn't touch your uncle's gun at all."

Mother: "It took me a lot of effort to wrestle it out of your hands. And now you say you didn't touch it?"

Father: "Well... what was I going to do?"

Mother: "Nothing serious! You just told me to bring a plane in front of the villa and fly you to Berlin so you could cook Hitler's goose and save the world, especially the lovers, from war. You were shouting and cursing Hitler and Göring with the most vulgar words."

Father: "Oh my son... I must have been dumbstruck. I don't remember saying such things."

Me: "Dad, were you really wasted?"

Father: "You sound just like your mother."

I couldn't answer him because my mother entered at that moment. She had been eavesdropping. She spoke to him so aggressively that he lost his nerve. But, worse than his state in that moment, was the fact that, in this argument, I had become the apple of my mother's eye— for proving I didn't fully believe my father's side of the story.

As she put it, my father had spent nearly three months—exactly 75 days—desperately trying to escape. But since all the paths and all the wells were under her control, he was caught every single time. He finally surrendered on August 15, 1945.

On that day, my mother went to his house alone. He was wearing long floral-print shorts and a T-shirt. He hadn't had time to change because, at that very moment, the radio had announced the news of the war's end. The female broadcaster declared that Emperor Hirohito's message would be aired in a few minutes. My mother sat on a blanket, leaned against a pillow, looked at my father with a sarcastic smile, and said: "Well, at least you don't need me to take you to the Gottardi War in Berlin anymore."

He sat there, dumbstruck, in the middle of the room. Before the emperor's message was broadcast, my mother asked, "So, what are you going to do? Will you come to the marriage registration office?"

He had no way out. He had to surrender. He finally agreed to go. But just as he opened his mouth to respond, the emperor's message was broadcast. His words and the emperor's words overlapped. In that moment, the emperor was also announcing Japan's unconditional surrender.

***

Unlike the unfortunate opponents of the fallen emperors—who later secured their status and power across the world—my mother soon realized that her victory was not a victory at all. It was meaningless. That is why, for years, she regretted the trick she had played. To be honest, I have never truly understood whether my mother had played tricks or if my father was the one to blame. Unfortunately, by the time I could seek the truth, it was too late. My father was lying in his grave forever, and I never had the courage to ask my mother.

My father soon became obsessed with gathering news and information about his so-called compassionate Emperor Hirohito. He never passed up a book or magazine that contained anything about the emperor. He even wrote two letters to him, but no matter how long he waited, he never received a response. Having translated the letters into English with the help of his friends, my father accused the emperor of not knowing any language other than Japanese. He believed that Hirohito simply hadn't understood what he had written. From time to time, he would even say: "It's a good thing the Japanese haven't entrusted him with running their country. Otherwise, instead of handling people's affairs, he would spend all his time tinkering with flowers in his greenhouse. If that were the case, the Japanese wouldn't be so progressive—they would be miserable and starving instead."

Neither my father nor my mother benefited from their marriage, but the worst part was that my mother had lost her wealthy suitors. Soon, she realized that all of my father's talk about his legendary inheritance had been nonsense. From then on, she sympathized with the defeated emperor even more than my father did.

My father worked as a reporter for *Dawn* Newspaper, and my mother was an employee of the Women's Organization. She was also a volunteer for sixteen different charities. Her efforts were admirable, especially in managing orphanages, supporting the families of prisoners, and even working with two militant organizations that aided both men and widows.

My father spent his days traveling around the city, gathering news for *Dawn* Newspaper. However, before submitting any article, he would always call my mother and ask for her opinion. He used to say: "At first, I just wanted your mother to help me correct my sentences.

But she outsmarted me—before I knew it, she became the chief editor of my news. She went even further, censoring anything she didn't like."

Thus, every morning, people across the country unknowingly read the news that my mother had approved. According to my father, he ran in circles every day, gathering information across the city, only for my mother to erase it in the blink of an eye. Of course, he had learned how to navigate his job well enough—he gathered more news than necessary, ensuring that even after my mother's censorship, he still had enough material left for the newspaper.

***

Then, something unexpected happened. The Ministry of Culture awarded my father the *Journalist of the Year* award, and he received it personally from the minister. It should have been a proud moment—something that would make even my mother happy. But the reason he was chosen was due to an article he had written about men's suicides, which, according to his report, were caused by the mistreatment of women. Somehow, my mother had overlooked this particular article. It sparked a massive public response across the country. Nearly 50,000 letters flooded the newspaper's office. The editor, unable to ignore such a reaction, publicly praised my father. He conducted an in-depth interview with him and even arranged for Ana Gilbert, an American photographer, to take flattering portraits of my father, which were published alongside the article. Soon, television and radio stations got involved. Our entire family spent days doing nothing but watching my father on TV or reading articles about him in various newspapers. My mother, furious, accused him of publishing the article without letting her read it first. He snapped: "I'll go get the original draft from the newspaper office—in your handwriting! Then I'll bring it to you. But mark my words, after that, I'll commit suicide—of course, only after writing a very controversial last will and testament!"

True to his word, he retrieved the article from the archives. Sure enough, it had been written in my mother's handwriting. Yet, she had no recollection of writing it. Now, it was his turn to mock her.

"While writing this, were you secretly searching for your uncle's gun to kill me?" he teased.

Although she was furious at his sarcasm, she had no choice but to back down. His threat of a dramatic last will and testament worried her. For days, she followed him around, step by step, terrified that he might actually snap and do something reckless.

Realizing how anxious she was, my father escalated his act. He played along so convincingly that after five days, my mother's nerves collapsed. She became so sick that we had to rush her to the hospital. Even in her weakened state, she still warned us to keep an eye on father.

However, when she saw how concerned he looked upon visiting her in the hospital, she realized he wasn't actually going to commit suicide.

For as long as he lived, my father never stopped cursing women—though always with absolute caution to ensure my mother didn't overhear him. But every time my mother filed for divorce, he suddenly fell ill. Twice, with the help of his friends, he even managed to get himself admitted to the CCU just long enough for the crisis to pass. Once the dust had settled, he would walk out—miraculously cured. My mother, on the other hand, seemed to be waiting for him to claim he had fully recovered just so she could bring up divorce again. Unable to fake another illness, my father eventually left the house in complete silence.

I vividly remember one night—we were all waiting for him to return for dinner. But he never came.

We had dinner and waited until midnight, but he still didn't show up. My mother called the *Dawn* Newspaper office, but the editor told her that my father had left work as usual and never returned. She began to panic. She called everyone she could think of—anyone who might have seen him. But nobody knew where he was. She didn't sleep a wink that night. At the break of dawn, she went to the newspaper office herself. My father hadn't come to work, nor had he taken any leave.

A second day passed. Still, there was no sign of him.

Desperate, my mother called the editor again. This time, he sounded genuinely worried. He suggested that she give him a photograph of my father so they could publish a missing person notice in the next day's newspaper. But my mother, in her growing agitation, refused. "Let's wait a little longer," she insisted. "Something will turn up."

Everyone in the house was consumed with anxiety—except for me. I didn't know where my father was, but strangely, I felt completely at ease. I had a gut feeling that nothing had happened to him. My mother, noticing my calmness, immediately suspected that my father and I had colluded somehow. She interrogated me for over an hour, searching for any clue that I might be hiding something. But she found nothing. Eventually, she stopped dosing social activities me and focused all her energy on searching for my father. But despite all her efforts, there was still no sign of him.

A week later, my father called from a city far away. Despite my mother's persistence, he refused to reveal the name of the city. She didn't believe him at all—partly because both he and the editor of *Dawn* Newspaper had been acting suspiciously. The editor called my mother several times a day, asking if we had any news about my father. However, the newspaper's Events Column continued to be filled with daily news, and its writing style and structure remained unchanged. It was still unmistakably his language—albeit polished with my mother's habitual edits and censorship, just as it had been for years.

Even though she could no longer alter his writing directly, her fingerprints were visible in every paragraph. This convinced her that my father and the editor had colluded and that he had never actually left the city. Determined to catch him red-handed, she borrowed a friend's car and concealed herself near the newspaper office for several days. But after hours of waiting and surveillance, she returned home exhausted and frustrated.

Two days after her return, my father called again. My mother begged him to come back. She insisted. But he told her he would return only when she changed her mind. She flew into a rage and hung up the phone. A week later, however, she had changed her mind. But by then, my father had stopped calling. His silence drove her mad.

Unlike my mother, I remained calm and unbothered. My composure irritated her. She accused me of secretly informing my father that she had softened. She tortured me day and night, trying to force a confession—demanding I reveal his hideout. But I had nothing to say.

Then, three months later, my father returned.

He arrived just as suddenly as he had left. The moment my mother saw him, she stood up and stormed into the bedroom in a sulky rage. My father, meanwhile, sat down in front of me—calm, triumphant, and silent. The glint of success was visible in his eyes.

A few days later, he told me he had been sent on a secret mission to the north. My mother, however, had archived every single issue of the newspaper from the past three months. She retrieved them, classified them, and meticulously combed through each page.

Her investigation uncovered a telling detail: in those three months, only 37 articles had been published about the north—far fewer than what one would expect from my father's supposed constant presence there. Convinced that he was lying, she berated him furiously.

Shortly after his return, my mother became pregnant.

When my sister found out, she confronted her: "Why would you get pregnant if you're planning to divorce him?"

My mother didn't answer. She was upset about it herself.

To this day, I don't know whose decision it was—hers or my father's. He also insisted that he didn't want another child.

Everyone, except me, turned against the unborn baby. I alone believed that its birth might be a mercy.

My sister was the most adamant. She pressured my mother to get an abortion and finally go through with the divorce. My mother's response was unexpected: "Damn this patriarchal society!"

We were stunned. Who had taught her to say that? She had never spoken like that before.

Eventually, she gave birth. But instead of celebrating, my father, my sister, and I all felt uneasy. Our new baby brother was—well—dim-witted. For the first time, my mother was the only one who wasn't upset. When I asked her why, she said: "He's the only one who will ever be happy in life, because he lacks wisdom and intelligence. He'll never worry about anything..." As time passed, her words proved true—especially considering the countless incidents that would later unfold.

***

My father was a kind and friendly man, especially toward me. Since I was a child, he took me out every evening. We often went to parks and cafés. At first, he would order a cup of Turkish coffee for himself and ice cream for me. As he sipped his coffee, he would reminisce. He shared his memories with me—not just any memories, but his memories of my mother. We always sat in a quiet spot, away from other people. He never censored his stories. He told me everything, even the things I was far too young to hear. Though I often blushed in embarrassment, I never complained, because I understood why he did it. He had two reasons. First, he wanted me to know my mother. It was as if he knew his time was running out. "I won't live long. I'll die. But you'll have to live with this woman for the rest of your life. You'd better understand her well." Second, he needed someone to confide in. And there was no one better than his son—his constant companion.

When we buried him, none of us knew whether it was he or my mother who was finally relieved. Perhaps both of them were. But what we did know was that, with my father gone, my mother's cruelty toward me and my sister only intensified. The one person she never tormented was our dim-witted brother. From that moment on, it became clear—he was happy. At least, for a while. He was so foolish—so mad—that when my mother oppressed us, we would turn to him for help. Of course, helping him was just an excuse. In truth, we needed his help. But my mother soon caught on. She learned our tricks. The moment she saw us approach our brother, she would shout: "Leave him alone! He doesn't need help! Don't use him as an excuse!"

And so, we were defenseless—standing before her without weapons or shields. We had no choice but to surrender.

That was when we realized—

Our father had been a good man.

And we had taken him for granted.

Chapter 2

Two years after my father's death, just a few days before the *Happiness Week* celebrations, I was in agony—as if suddenly experiencing the pain of childbirth. I knew something was going to happen. From the very beginning, I kept a close eye on my mother, but unlike my father, she remained safe and sound. My sister also lived as if nothing had changed from the previous days. I wasn't worried about my brother. As my mother had always said, he was supposed to be the lucky one among us. At that time, he was seven years old. If something bad happened to him, it would prove my mother's prediction wrong.

I anxiously awaited the first day of *Happiness Week*. Once or twice, I asked my sister to check on our mother and see if she was upset. But she only scolded me, calling me an owl, and said: "Mom's fine. You'd better take care of yourself. Your time has come."

As she spoke, I stared at her face—she looked pale. Suddenly, I feared that she was the one in danger. Unfortunately, I couldn't talk to my mother. She had left on a trip two days ago. I was torn between my worries about her and my concerns for my sister.

This time, calamity struck sooner than I expected.

I sensed it immediately on the morning of the first day of *Happiness Week*. My sister was leaving the house, her brows furrowed, her lips pouted. I advised her, "Don't go out looking like that. You should be laughing from the bottom of your heart." But she snapped, "I'm not in the mood for laughing." Then, just as we reached the door, she confessed—she had fallen in love. At first, I thought this meant they would get married and that *Happiness Week* would be even happier for us than for anyone else.

But when she returned home, she was even more depressed than before. It had all been wishful thinking. Her boyfriend hadn't taken the bait. Perhaps he had absconded. And with our mother gone, we had no idea what to do. She had left on a journey with her group of oppressed widows. Or rather, they claimed to be oppressed. I swear to God, the real oppressed ones were those buried beneath the earth—those whose sighs from the grave still caused the ground above them to sink every day.

My sister and I decided to talk to her boyfriend. He wasn't in his office. My sister described him as a tall, broad-shouldered man. But more than that, he was what she called a four-hybrid boy—his mother and father were both of mixed backgrounds, with no compatible genes between them. His father was Armenian and Georgian. His mother was Turkish and Arab. A genetic concoction, impossible to categorize. He would say one thing on the phone, then forget it an hour later. If we made an appointment, he would wait for us several streets away from the agreed-upon location.

He seemed confused—dumb, even.

I asked my sister, "How do you expect to live with this madman?"

She defended him, "He has fooled you. He isn't insane—he's actually very clever. Smarter than both you and me. And more cautious, too."

When the time came for the final conversation with him, despite my sister's insistence that this was her problem to solve alone, I refused to let her go alone—especially while our mother was away.

Yes, it was her business. It was none of mine. But, to be honest, I was afraid. Afraid that he would hurt her. If anything happened to her, we would be the ones in trouble—especially during *Happiness Week*. So this time, my sister relented and took me along. We arrived at his office without an appointment. And the moment I saw him, I felt as if Othello himself was standing before me. He had a square, blurry face, a broad nose, and two large eyes that sat too far apart. He was massive—so giant and heavy that I turned and glanced at my sister. Standing next to him, she looked like a little girl beside her father. Not in terms of age, but in size. In fact, she even seemed older than him. But the moment he spoke, I almost burst into laughter. His voice did not match his physique. It was soft. Feminine. And that wasn't even the biggest problem. The real problem was that we couldn't understand a word he said. He spoke with a mix of Georgian, Turkish, Armenian, and Arabic accents, blending them together into an indecipherable concoction. I leaned forward and whispered into my sister's ear: "My dear Desdemona... it's best to forget him. He's not worth ruining your life over."

She frowned. "Where are your manners? What the hell is Desdemona?"

I smirked. "Look at him. He's Othello himself."

She lowered her head and covered her mouth with her hand to hide her laughter. Then she whispered back: "So... you're saying I should let him get away?"

I shrugged. "At least get something out of him first. Then let him go."

She sighed. "He doesn't give me much money now. But once he realizes he's in love with me, he'll pay through the nose."

That day, we left Othello's office frustrated. Not because he refused to give in—he had relented and was trying to work things out. But the truth was... We simply couldn't understand him. On the way home, I scolded my sister. "Where on earth did you even meet that strange man?" She didn't answer. She just leaned against the seat, staring out the window in silence.

I sent a telegram to my mother immediately. At the time, she was staying in a hotel near the hot springs, where all forty-two widows were soaking in sulfurous water. She received my message that same day and called me from her hotel room. She advised my sister, "Don't get yourself into any more trouble. Kick that multi-hybrid boy to the curb and be done with him. If I had done the same with your father, we'd all be happy right now."

My sister listened intently. But she didn't admit anything. When I told my mother to ask her where she had met that devil, my sister lost her temper. "It's my business. I don't need anyone's help. Especially not from our idiot brother!"

And with that, the conversation was over.

***

My sister is a mixture of both mother and father in appearance. Her eyes were gray, and her skin was fair— brighter than our mother's. However, her facial features were well-proportioned, like our father's. From the very beginning, we all knew that if she never faced adversity, she would grow into a beautiful woman.

Our mother doted on her, wrapping her in cotton wool. My sister had been exercising ever since she was aware of herself. In high school, she became a marathon champion. We all believed she had a bright future ahead. But after graduating, she suddenly stopped exercising.

Our parents were resentful. No matter how much they urged her to continue, she refused and instead started searching for a job.

She was always cheeky and stubborn.

After high school, she took a job at an accident and emergency hospital—on the other side of the city. It might as well have been a whole other city; it was that far.

I vividly remember my mother begging her to quit. "You could find a job at a hospital closer to home," she said. "With the help of my friends and acquaintances, I could arrange it." But my sister made excuses. "I don't want to be in anyone's debt."

She left for work early in the morning and came home late at night. I never fully realized how far the hospital was until the day I broke my leg in an accident. They took me to that same accident and emergency hospital. Before the doctor could examine my leg, I asked a nurse to call my sister. The nurse frowned, but she called her anyway. My sister arrived quickly and stood beside the doctor as he scanned my leg and put it in a cast. Unlike the nurse, the doctor was thrilled to see my sister. I noticed the joy on his face. I was watching her closely to see what she would do. But I wasn't the only one watching—he had also noticed my gaze. I think my nosiness annoyed him, because when he moved my leg, he twisted it so badly that I screamed in pain. After finishing their work, they took me to the fourth floor and left me alone. The room was gloomy and silent. I was the only patient there. If I had even one other patient to talk to, I wouldn't have gotten so bored. But

I had no choice. I couldn't move. I stared at the walls. At the door. Until I drifted into sleep. Just as my eyelids were closing, my sister walked in. Her face was flushed. I wanted to ask why she had left me alone, but I decided against it. She had already helped me. That was enough. I couldn't expect too much from her. She wasn't the hospital's manager—just a nurse, like hundreds of others. The doctors liked her only because of her good manners.

She wore her white uniform and took care of me every day. That was when I realized just how important she was at the hospital. Even in her absence, the nurses brought me anything I requested—immediately.

Yet, despite her high status, she was suddenly fired by the head of the hospital. Three months after my accident, she lost her job. Some doctors intervened, and she was transferred to Hospital No. 5—which, luckily, was near our house. At the time, our father was still alive, and he was a well-known reporter of city incidents. Both my parents were pleased about my sister's new job. But my sister was miserable. The moment she got home, she would grab the telephone and curse the head of her previous hospital. I used to think she was polite, but those days made me realize what a storehouse of profanity she carried in her mind. The creative insults she shouted over the phone shocked even me.

Of course, I had no right to interfere in her business—just as she had no right to interfere in mine. She made that clear, and I had accepted it. I interfered neither in her business nor in my mother's—just as they had no right to interfere in mine. Still, I often overheard my mother warning her about what people were saying behind her back. My sister just shrugged. "Fuck their fathers," she said. "Let them do whatever they want. They're worse than me. No matter what you do, they'll always talk nonsense. Do we live for them? If their hearts are burning, they should get some water and put out the fire themselves."

Despite the doctors' support, my sister lasted only a few months at Hospital No. 5 before getting fired again. This time, she wasn't transferred anywhere—just terminated outright. After that, she hopped from job to job, each completely different from the last. Her work history was so diverse that I sometimes thought she had as much experience as an entire office building. But the only job she held for any significant period was at a hair salon. She claimed she curled hair, but months later, I was convinced she had lied.

One day, when she offered to curl my mother's hair, I realized—she didn't even know what curly hair was.

Either my sister was a talentless fraud, or she had been doing something else at that salon.

She botched my mother's hair so badly that when my mother looked in the mirror, she gasped: "What exactly do you do at that hair salon?! Someone who has never set foot in a salon curls hair better than you! Really, what do you even do at the salon?"

Sister said, "Your hair curls badly. If you were young, you'd see how well I could curl it."

Mother shook her head in disappointment and went to her usual salon to get her hair curled. I didn't understand why she even needed curls at her age. She had reached an age where curls no longer suited her. Well, I made a mistake trying to advise her.

Mother angrily yelled at me and my sister, accusing us of deliberately trying to make her look older.

Sister went to the salon every day until one day she came home and said she had argued with the salon owner and refused to work there anymore. Mother wanted to go and talk to the owner, but sister insisted she would never set foot in that place again and that mother should also stay away. No matter how much mother tried to advise her, sister wouldn't listen. In the end, mother pouted in frustration and backed down.

My sister rested at home for three days. During this time, the phone rang non-stop, making such a racket that it got on my nerves. I had no choice but to leave the house and go to my friend's place. But even there, I couldn't stay because my friend had gone on a work assignment.

I returned home. Mother was telling sister about the awful things being said behind her back. But, of course, she added, "I know my daughter well. People are just talking nonsense. It's those who have failed in their own work and are jealous, trying to sabotage my daughter."

Through a series of phone calls, she got hired as a secretary for a commercial company that imported plastic gloves and other similar products. Her salary was significantly higher than what she earned at the salon. She bragged that it was because of her skills and experience as a secretary. I laughed in her face. "Don't lie to me. You don't even know what a secretary does."

She tried to justify herself. To be honest, I wasn't convinced. But I was tired of arguing with her, so I let it go. However, two months later, she was fired again. This time, even my mother admitted I had been right all along. Still, she told me, "Let's not make a big deal out of it. It doesn't matter what happened. She doesn't work there anymore."

Over the next year, my sister cycled through so many jobs that I lost count. I asked her how she managed to endure all those different roles. She just shrugged. "I don't care what I do or who I deal with. I only care about the money. The more, the better."

It was at one of those jobs that she met Othello.

And from there, everything changed.

***

Finally, the Eastern Othello gave in and agreed to pay my sister a king's ransom to get her off his back. Of course, he denied making such a promise until the very last moment, but my sister had enough leverage, and her persistence forced him to pay through the nose just to rid himself of such a stubborn and intrusive girl.

The sum he finally offered was staggering. Even my mother—who was still closely monitoring the whole ordeal—and I were left shocked.

But my sister warned us: "This is my personal matter. I can handle it myself. It's best if you don't interfere." The Eastern Othello was absolutely stunned when he realized that the greedy Desdemona had no intention of compromising.

Our family crisis had reached such a boiling point that my mother cut her trip short and returned home. It was now three against one—my mother, myself, and even Othello—against my sister alone. But she stood her ground. I didn't dare say much; I only participated in the voting. But my sister, like a powerful minority that always finds a way to rule, won again.

The constant conflict and arguments left us all so exhausted that we barely noticed when *Happiness Week* came to an end. We had been so busy dealing with our own mess that we had no idea what had been happening outside. Only my mother still left the house for daily shopping. But she was so angry with my sister that she walked the entire distance—from home to the shops and back—frowning the whole way. "I haven't even heard the sound of people celebrating once," she complained.

The day after *Happiness Week*, a police officer arrived—and arrested all four of us. Once again, our silly brother's good luck was proven. My mother, sister, Othello, and I followed the officer to the police station. There, an elderly officer, clearly nearing retirement, pulled out our case file. He lectured us on all the deficiencies in our special ceremonies. No matter how much my mother and my sister's future husband tried to reason with him, he refused to budge. He was as obstinate as my sister. Eventually, he sent us to court. The judge, who was just as old as the officer, didn't care about anything we had to say. Each of us was sentenced to 15 days in prison and ordered to pay heavy fines.

That was when my sister snapped.

She grabbed Othello by the collar and shouted: "This is your fault! If you had just given in, we could have held a ceremony, joined the public celebrations, and maybe even won a special prize!

My mother rolled her eyes and cut her off. "Damn the special prize. What do you plan to do with this misfortune?" After some more arguing, my mother and sister forced the Eastern Othello to not only pay our fines but also buy our 60-day prison sentences. The sum was so enormous that it meant the world to him. Of course, we still had to spend one night in jail until he finalized the payments. That night, we even had a visitor—our lucky brother. He showed up cheerfully with a basket of fruit, as if we were in need of extra vitamins for our 15-day imprisonment. Of course, we never received the fruit. By morning, Othello had paid our way out, and we returned home with our lucky brother.

***

After my father's passing, another man joined our family—my sister's husband. However, he was immediately dissatisfied with the house's limited space and its old doors. As soon as he settled in, he started complaining. Finally, after two months, he bought a new house—one closer to the accident and emergency hospital where my sister used to work.

In this new neighborhood, no one knew us. We were finally free from our nosy old neighbors. On top of that, we now owned a car. My sister quit her string of jobs and became the supervisor of her husband's several companies. Since she had to travel between offices, she needed a car for inspections and meetings. She left home early in the morning, just like she did when she was single. She supervised the northern companies until noon, then returned home for lunch—which my mother cooked. After a short rest, she left again, this time overseeing the southern companies until dusk.

***

The days passed peacefully. Nobody complained—not even my sister's husband. Of course, even if he was unhappy about something, he never said anything. Only my mother continued to take care of everyone.

One evening, we all went to a country restaurant on the hillside. Over dinner, my mother told my sister that she should cut back on work since she was becoming thinner by the day. My sister's husband immediately agreed. But my sister refused. That was when I realized—he wasn't really concerned about her health. He wasn't happy with her supervision of his companies, and he was looking for an excuse. And this was the best one he could find. Just like during the wedding discussions, we were all on one side, and she was on the other. And, once again, the minority won.

We left the restaurant late at night. The street was narrow and quiet, sloping downward. My sister's husband drove fast. Before reaching the square, we heard a car honking behind us. At first, we thought it was just trying to overtake us. My sister's husband glanced at the rearview mirror, then pulled over and stopped. The car drove ahead, parked, and we saw—it was a police car. Two officers got out. It was as if they had been hand-picked to be opposites—one was extremely fat, while the other was so slim he looked like he might faint. My sister's husband stepped out of the car to speak with them. Their car was fifty meters away from ours—or rather, my sister's car—so we couldn't hear their conversation. They spoke for a long time. Finally, my sister got out and walked toward them. But before she could say a word, her husband waved her off, telling her to go back. He continued talking to the officers alone. Half an hour later, he returned—looking like a beaten man. "They told me to follow their car to the police station," he said.

Apparently, our peaceful dinner had been deemed a feast. And, according to the officers, holding a feast was a crime. At the police station, we quickly realized what was going on—the special mourning ceremony had begun. We were lined up on a long, narrow bench, all sitting in a row. An officer sat at a desk in front of us. He did not speak to us. Not because he was a coward or cruel—but because his phones were ringing non-stop. He picked them up with both hands, switching between calls. Behind him was a glass wall, and through it, we could see officers sitting in front of a row of computers. They were either too fat or too thin—sitting in an alternating pattern, as if arranged deliberately. One of the officers who had brought us in told us to wait for the guard officer. But there was no sign of him. An hour passed. Still, no one came to see us. There was no explanation. We didn't ask questions—we just waited. Eventually, we fell asleep. Only my lucky brother got special permission to lie down on one of the benches. Another sign of his endless luck and happiness.

When the guard officer finally entered, the waiting room erupted in noise. A group of agents followed behind him. We startled. But the guard officer was in no hurry. He was so fat that he could barely walk. He strolled to his office, closed the door, and ignored us completely. So, we went back to waiting. Half an hour later, the guard officer finally emerged. He lined us up and led us through a small door built into the glass wall. Inside was a hall lined with computers. That was when we realized—these were the same computers my sister's husband had sold to the police station. His employees inspected them every month. Thanks to the high quality of his products, our case files appeared on the screen with just a few keystrokes. There were countless cases of rebelling against special ceremonies. But this time, there were so many violations that the guard officer shook his head in disappointment as he read through the list of our offenses.

The court doubled both our fines and our prison sentence. But we didn't panic. Why? Because my sister's husband was there. And he paid for everything—again. According to my mother, he was to blame for the whole mess anyway. "If he hadn't invited us to dinner, we would have been home. There would have been no fines. No prison." And since he blamed himself, he paid—without a word, without a frown.

As soon as we arrived home, my sister declared that nobody was allowed to leave the house until the weekend. We all obeyed—inevitably. Even her husband, despite being deeply worried about the affairs of his companies, followed her orders without question. However, two days before the weekend, my sister fell ill. She felt dizzy and nauseous. My mother took her to the hospital, and we all waited anxiously for their return. When they finally came back, we realized—my sister was pregnant. Although she and my mother were thrilled, they pretended to be devastated out of fear. But the moment they walked through the door, their true emotions surfaced, and they couldn't hide their joy. Her husband, beaming, clapped his hands together and said:

"The *Mourning Week* isn't over yet, and holding feasts is forbidden... but let's go to a restaurant! My treat!" Everyone agreed—except for my lucky brother. Despite our insistence, he refused to join us. "I'm not in the mood to spend another night on a police station bench," he said flatly. And with that, he avoided the feast. We left without him.

The moment my lucky brother declined the invitation, I felt a shock run through me. Then, my stomach twisted with anxiety. My animal instinct kicked in again. But my mind refused to process what was coming. Well, my sister's husband—and his wallet full of money, which could have solved the problems—were involved, but the feeling was too strong to ignore. I turned to my mother and hesitated before saying: "Maybe we should skip the feast." She said: "Getting arrested is inevitable. But your sister's husband will take care of it—just like he did twice before."

She had become bolder—almost reckless. I said nothing more and simply followed them. As we walked out of the yard, I turned back for a moment and saw my lucky brother watching us through the window. Before stepping through the gate, I paused—staring at him with envy.

That night, my sister's husband was driving again. We went to The *Black Cat* Restaurant—a famous, expensive place in the newly built *Pearl Neighborhood*. The moment I saw the name of the restaurant, my heart clenched. But I tried to calm myself. I didn't want to hear my sister mock me for being superstitious. They had already given me enough nicknames—I didn't need another one. Everyone else was talking and laughing, enjoying the night. But my anxiety only grew. I kept looking around—frantically scanning the restaurant, the staff, the other diners. I saw no signs of trouble. Everything seemed fine. I tried—several times—to relax and enjoy myself like the rest of them. I reminded myself that we already knew how this would end: arrest. But that wasn't the real issue. My sister's husband had assured us that he would fix everything. I even pictured the entire scene—Us sitting in the police station, him smirking at the guard officer, tossing the receipt of our fines onto the judge's table, and winking at us as he said, "Let's go." I tried to entertain myself with these thoughts. But my anxiety refused to leave. My mother noticed. Several times during the meal, she gestured at me—her way of saying, "Calm down." But it didn't work. Finally, she stood up and pretended to head to the bathroom. As she passed by me, she leaned down and whispered: "Your sister's husband is here. What's eating you? Enjoy yourself. Worst case, we spend one night in the police station. One night isn't the rest of your life." I wanted to correct her—she had butchered the proverb.

But before I could speak, she walked away and rejoined my sister and her husband.

We stayed at the restaurant late. By the time we left, it was past midnight, and we were the last customers to go. We weren't in a hurry—it was almost as if we wanted to stay there forever, to prolong the night rather than spend it on the benches of the police station. We knew what was coming. We expected to be arrested—but not yet. We walked slowly to the car, waiting for the police to overtake us down the street. We did not expect them to arrest us before we even got in the car. Two officers approached. Each held a walkie-talkie in their hands. They walked straight toward my sister's husband. One of them said, "We have orders to prevent you or your companions from driving." Then, the police officer himself got behind the wheel. My sister's husband didn't say a word. And just like that, we were on our way—to the police station.

The guard officer, who was old, knew my sister's husband well—after all, he had purchased all the police station's equipment from him, from computers to pushpins on the desk. A slim officer tapped at the computer keyboard with his thin, bony fingers, printing out copies of our case files. As he walked toward the guard officer's room, he glanced at us with pity. That was when I realized—our happy day, or rather, our happy night, was about to have an unhappy ending.

The guard officer read through our files. Then, he looked up and said bluntly, "There will be no forgiveness this time. You will pay the fines and serve your prison sentences." He added that strict enforcement was necessary because of our repeat offenses. My mother was completely defeated. No matter how much I tried to talk to her, she ignored me and told me to shut up—more out of exhaustion than anything else. That night, we remained in the police station until morning. However, instead of sitting on wooden benches, the commander took pity on us and led us to a room with empty beds, handing each of us a gray military blanket. Given our situation, that small act of mercy felt like a miracle—especially considering what was waiting for us in court the following day. My mother and sister lay down and fell asleep quickly. My sister's husband paced the room for half an hour before finally deciding he needed to conserve his energy for court the next day. He collapsed onto the bed nearest the window. I, however, could neither sleep nor lie down. That night, I despised my mother. She had dragged us into this mess. If only I hadn't let her lead me by the nose. If only I had been a foolish disciple of my crazy brother. Then, I would have been at home, sleeping soundly in my own bed, just like the three people who were now resting peacefully around me.

At dawn, they lined us up and transported us to court in a rusty old Jeep. Unlike our previous trials, this time, the judge was a young man. At first, he gave us a disgusted glare. Then, he lectured us: "You are lawbreakers—people who disrespect traditions and care nothing for special ceremonies. You showed grief during *Happiness Week*, and you held a feast during *Mourning Week*. You break the laws and disrupt society whenever you get the chance!"

He talked a lot. But none of us were in the mood to listen. Even the judge's secretary—a middle-aged man—was dozing off. Unfortunately, it was either our bad luck or his that the judge turned and noticed him. All of a sudden, the judge lost interest in his speech. His voice softened, and his lecture abruptly ended. Instead, he hastily read out the verdict, fumbling over the words.

The fines had been doubled. Well—so what? It wasn't like we were going bankrupt. My sister's husband was going to pay. But what about our two-month prison sentence? That couldn't be bought off. That was when my sister's husband stood up and announced: "My wife is pregnant. She cannot go to jail." The judge barely looked at him. He scribbled a note, handed it to a police officer, and ordered them to take my sister to the police laboratory for confirmation. Then, without another word, he turned back to his next case. We left the courtroom and waited for my sister and the police officer to return. Hours passed. Sunset came, and still they were gone. By the time they finally returned, the judge had already left for the day. With no other option, the police officers escorted us back to the police station. At the station, my sister pulled my mother aside and whispered: "I bribed the officer to take me for a big lunch before going to the lab." Then, she smirked. "The idiot didn't want to finish his mission, so he took the longest possible route. We drove through half the city before he finally took me to the lab." She shook her head. "I still don't know if he was stupid or just stalling on purpose."

The next day, the judge examined the lab results. Without saying a word, he used his authority to strike out the unpurchaseable word from my sister's verdict. She was free to go. The rest of us were sent to prison.

My mother was placed in the women's jail. My sister's husband and I were thrown into the muggers' cell. We were the only two prisoners who received daily visits. Every single day, our lucky brother brought us cigarettes and fruit to get through the day. And twice a week, my sister came along with him.

***

We were allowed to visit our mother only once during the two months of her imprisonment. Unlike my sister's husband and me, my mother never complained about her cell. In fact, she believed that getting acquainted with the seven other women in her cell had been immensely useful. She said those women had been arrested for burglary in broad daylight. And thanks to them, she had learned a great deal about how burglars broke into houses. "I've gained so much experience," she told us proudly. "I could insure our house against every possible trick used by those tramps—without having to pay a single cent to the extortionist insurance industry!"

***

When we were finally released from prison, my sister and our lucky brother were waiting for us at the gate. Both of them had gained weight. At first, we were surprised. Then, we realized—my brother's obesity was due to gluttony, while my sister had simply swollen because of the growing baby in her stomach.

We rested for a week after our release. Then, I told my mother, "I need to find a job. I'm tired of being unemployed." But there was a problem— The two-month prison sentence on my record. No company would hire someone with so many legal violations that the court had been forced to impose the harshest penalty available. My mother, however, dismissed my concerns. "There's nothing to be sad about," she said. "We don't need to work for other people. With our status, it would be beneath our dignity to work for someone else." That was all she had to say. As soon as she was finished, my sister signaled at me to follow her. We went straight to her husband's headquarters. I didn't like the idea of working in his office. And, fortunately, my sister's husband didn't want me around either. He wanted me out of sight. So, he sent me off to one of his remote companies, located just off the West Highway, while he stayed in his city-center office and continued his work— undisturbed. But I wasn't upset about it. In fact, I was relieved. I preferred working away from him. He got rid of a nuisance—and so did I. All I wanted was a job that would allow me to earn as much money as I needed. It didn't matter where the money came from or how I earned it.

***

Life became calm and peaceful. But sometimes, I worried about my sister's delivery. I was afraid she might give birth during *Mourning Week*. If that happened, we would have to pretend we had lost the baby. It was her first child, and my mother's first grandchild— And, knowing them, they would accidentally slip up and burst out laughing at the wrong moment. So, I sat down and calculated the exact date of my sister's delivery. It turned out she would give birth two months and ten days before *Mourning Week*, right in the middle of *Happiness Week*. That thrilled me. I showed my sister the sheet of paper where I had done the calculations. She took it and checked my math carefully with her husband and a calendar. Her husband frowned, then said, "You've made a mistake—you counted the pregnancy two days longer than it actually is. To be precise, it's two months and twelve days before *Mourning Week*. Even if she delivers a little early or a little late, the baby will still be born at least two and a half months before or at worst

two months and a week before the mourning period."
That was a relief to all of us—Except for our lucky
brother, of course. He was already relaxed. Nothing ever
worried him. Nothing ever happened to him. He
remained completely untouched by all of our family's
troubles and hardships. His natural-born luck shielded
him from everything. It carried him effortlessly through
life, overcoming any obstacles in his way.

I worked at the new company for a month. Then, as my
sister's pregnancy progressed, she could no longer
handle her work as before. So, her duties were passed on
to me. That meant I was now responsible for
supervising all of her husband's companies. Meanwhile,
my mother became my sister's personal nurse. Since my
new responsibilities required a lot of traveling, I took my
sister's car. At first, I was thrilled. Then, after a few days,
I realized just how difficult her job had been. I couldn't
believe how she had managed for so long. One had to be
exceptionally tough to handle this kind of work without
breaking down. I drove non-stop from morning to
evening, but at least I didn't have to rush home for lunch
like she did. Nobody was waiting for me at home. So, I
just ate out.

***

My sister gave birth to her baby two days before *Happiness Week*. The baby was a boy—and he was heavy. So heavy, in fact, that he looked completely mismatched with my sister's small frame. For a moment, we all thought the hospital had accidentally swapped him with another baby. Besides his weight, he didn't resemble my sister or her husband at all. But my mother dismissed our concerns immediately. "Babies change over the first few months," she said. That was enough to relieve my sister's husband. Despite the baby's unexpected size, we were all happy to welcome a new member into the family. However, I still had a butterfly in my stomach. The unease that had troubled me the previous week refused to leave. Even after the birth, when I walked into my sister's room and saw her holding her son, I felt only partially relieved. Something still felt off. We discharged my sister on the first day of *Happiness Week* and took her home. She was extremely weak. Her breathing was shallow and wheezing. Her hollow eyes and protruding cheekbones made her look even frailer. The doctor had already given her two units of blood, but she still needed two more. But I wasn't worried about that. She was home—and her husband was staying with her. Meanwhile, he told me to go supervise all the companies in his absence. Feeling reassured about my sister's condition, I walked through the streets humming happy songs, smiling at everyone I passed. That day, I stopped at three red lights, rolled down the car window, and told recent jokes I had heard. Not only did the police officers laugh, but even the drivers on both sides of me joined in. One of the officers seemed to recognize me—his eyes widened in surprise. Perhaps he had expected me to look miserable so he could arrest me again. It had always been that way before. But that year, during *Happiness Week*, my family members were happier than anyone else—and, for once, we had a real reason to be.

I returned home at 9:30 at night. I was exhausted. My head ached, and my back throbbed. But when I walked inside, I noticed that my sister, mother, and her husband were gone. Only my lucky brother was home. "Where is everyone?" I asked. "Mom and sister's husband took sister back to the hospital," he said. I felt a wave of unease wash over me. I was worried about my sister. But, at the same time, I was terrified of making a mistake—it was, after all, the first day of *Happiness Week*. Given my already long record of offenses, I knew that any trouble this time wouldn't be easily forgiven. I could be sentenced to more than two months in prison. On the one hand, I was alone, which meant I couldn't rely on my sister's husband to pay my fines. On the other hand, my mother and sister's husband were in even worse shape than I was. They stood in front of my sister's hospital room, chatting and laughing loudly. They looked as if they were waiting outside a bride's bedroom, anticipating good news. When I walked toward them, they turned to face me, still in high spirits. I could tell they were discussing my sister's condition—which was clearly not good. But since they had to obey the rules of *Happiness Week*, they maintained their joyful façade.

My sister remained in the hospital for a full week. With my mother and the nurses taking care of her, she eventually recovered—returning to the way she had been before giving birth. Only her pale face remained as a reminder of her struggles. But it wasn't anything serious. Since she had no reason to go out, she stayed home, resting and regaining her strength. Soon, her health improved, and the roses returned to her cheeks. But none of that concerned me much. The real blessing was that my sister had recovered, and we hadn't been dragged into another disaster. We had barely escaped trouble this time. Of course, I wasn't worried about my sister's physical health—I was worried that we might slip up and give people an excuse to turn us in. But, in the end, my sister was in pain, her husband spent money, and my mother took care of her. It was none of my business.

We were all relieved, and my sister's husband, overjoyed at her recovery, suggested: "Let's go to a restaurant to celebrate!" We immediately refused. We weren't willing to risk trouble again. "We can't afford another mistake," we told him. We knew we could easily slip up and get caught—even if it was inadvertently. So, he changed his mind, and we held a small celebration at home instead. As the party began, my lucky brother excused himself and went to his bedroom. At first, my mother thought he had gone to get something. But when he didn't return, she went to fetch him. Moments later, she came back alone. "He's asleep," she told my sister. "Like a rock." A shiver ran down my spine. What if something was about to happen? And once again, our lucky brother would escape it completely? Suddenly, the celebration lost all meaning for me. I spent the rest of the night watching the door to his bedroom and the front door of the house.

But—

Nothing happened.

By morning, I realized I had worried for nothing. And so, I cursed that silly, lucky boy— For ruining the party for me. For messing up my night. All because of his damn untimely sleep.

Chapter 3

Different events took place and changed the atmosphere of our home. Mother, who had gained some freedom after my sister's childbirth, became more socially active. However, this time, her activities had taken a different turn. At first, I was suspicious because her newfound interests did not align with her limited literacy and knowledge. Out of the blue, she had become politically engaged, and her conversations were filled with political discussions. We couldn't figure out what she was involved in. In other words, we had no idea who had put such ideas into her head. We knew all her friends well. None of them—neither the women nor the men—were the type to discuss such matters. My sister suggested that she might have made new acquaintances or that perhaps a man was influencing her. I needed help to understand what was really going on with my mother, but quitting my job to follow her around was not an option. Unfortunately, there was no one I could turn to. My fortunate brother had more free time than anyone else, yet he remained detached, as if he were exempt from our struggles and problems. I couldn't count on him. My sister's husband was also extremely busy, preoccupied with his own affairs. Worse still, as a new addition to our family, we couldn't ask him to follow our mother and uncover her secret. The only person who could do it was my sister. I thought she could place her infant in a basket on the car seat and keep an eye on Mother. But when I suggested it, she simply shrugged and said, "It has nothing to do with you. Why do you try to act as a proxy for others? It's none of your business what she does."

I had to admit she had a point. I wasn't trying to spy on or trouble Mother—I only wanted to ensure that she wasn't in any danger. Yet something gnawed at me. I kept thinking about what my sister had said. A person's choices are their own responsibility, but in the end, we could all end up entangled in Mother's problems. On the other hand, I wasn't the kind of person to abandon her in difficult times like a stranger and say, "It's none of my business."

Days passed, and Mother continued her political rants. We couldn't determine whether she supported the *Independence Party* or the *Stability Party*. One day, she would repeat the slogans of the *Independence Party*, and the next day, she would parrot those of the *Stability Party*.

Both parties had recently set up offices in different corners of the city, and their leaders were beginning to stir unrest. Although I was overwhelmed with work and exhausted, I had overheard some of their speeches. Since they failed to impress me, I quickly dismissed them from my mind.

At first, Mother would recite slogans she had read on the city walls, and we didn't pay much attention. But then, she started speaking with a certain logic and conviction. That's when we realized she was in league with someone. As I had suspected all along, something was going on— yet nobody else seemed to notice, except me.

One day, she entered the house and announced that we had to enroll in one of the political parties.

She didn't specify which party. I was the first in the family to oppose her, but my sister's husband objected, saying that we should at least listen to what she had to say before rejecting the idea if it wasn't logical.

Mother, emboldened by his support, declared, "This is the era of political parties and associations. We mustn't ignore it."

I stared at her in disbelief. When she noticed my expression, she snapped, "Why are you looking at me like that? Am I lying?"

I replied, "The issue isn't whether you're lying or not. I just want to know where you learned all of this. These words aren't yours."

Her face flushed with anger as she accused me of slandering her. That was never my intention. There was no slander in my mind, but no matter how hard I tried to explain, she refused to understand. My words went unheard, drowned out by her shouting and screaming. Finally, my sister and her husband intervened, raising their voices in protest, and she fell silent.

I was so angry that my whole body started to tremble. At that moment, I felt as if a disaster was about to unfold— the catastrophe I had feared ever since my mother began speaking about politics.

I looked around. She was still glaring at me with fury. My sister was quietly gathering the items on the table. Her husband had pulled out a cigarette and was searching for his lighter, which had fallen onto the carpet. And my fortunate brother? He sat calmly, absentmindedly playing with his fingers. I was certain he hadn't even registered our argument. His serenity was absolute, and I envied him—I wished I had been born oblivious to it all.

The political debate wasn't over, but it had escalated. My sister's husband only made things worse. His first argument was about prioritizing the parties. He believed we needed to determine which party had a brighter future before deciding to join. We were expected to present our reasons and then draw a conclusion.

Mother spoke first. That was when we realized she was a supporter of the *Stability Party*. I had assumed she opposed it, especially given her past criticisms of patriarchy. But her reasons for favoring that party were weak. She said, "Our country isn't under foreign control, so why should we demand freedom? In these times of instability and unrest, the most important thing is stability."

Although she was right, I started to oppose her because I believed her speech would have consequences. My reasoning was just as simple as hers in that discussion— I was merely trying to disrupt her entire argument. As she spoke, I picked up a sheet of paper and pretended to take notes, though, in reality, I was searching my mind for a counterargument. Despite the nervous flutter in my stomach, a thought suddenly crossed my mind.

I glanced at her. She had finished speaking and was now leaning back on the sofa, looking around with a triumphant expression. Her face radiated happiness, and in that moment, she appeared more beautiful. Though I admired her confidence, I secretly laughed at her, knowing that her victory would be short-lived. She seemed to sense what I was about to do, as her face twitched and her smile faded.

I thought to myself, Now is the perfect time for a counteroffensive. I began, "It's true that our country isn't under foreign control and that we are an independent nation. I agree that stability is essential in this world, and I accept all of that. But that doesn't mean we should sacrifice our freedom. Mother herself has said that nothing in this world is truly stable. So, doesn't that mean our freedom could also be lost? The founders of the *Independence Party* recognized this issue, which is why they established the party in the first place."

My sister's husband, sitting across from me on the sofa, listened intently. Unlike before, he did not oppose me. Instead, after I finished speaking, he clapped. With that, I had weakened Mother's position. Nobody bothered to ask my lucky brother for his opinion. That left only my sister, and if she sided with Mother, I still wouldn't lose—we would at least be tied at 2–2. And that's exactly what happened. As always, my sister took Mother's side and opposed me. Of course, I suspected she did this out of spite, to make up for the time I had opposed her when she was trying to free herself from the Eastern Othello. Well, democracy had once again shown me its ugly side. We had no choice but to accept her vote, even though she contributed nothing new to the discussion. She simply repeated Mother's arguments, and before I knew it, a women's parliamentary party had formed against the men in our household. This deepened my resentment toward my lucky brother. If he had been a proper participant, capable of voting, our side would have won—three votes to two. We would have had the final say. At that moment, my sister glanced at her son. A sarcastic remark formed in my mind, one that would wipe the smile off her face. I said, "Don't bring your son into the discussion. He's far too young. He can't even speak, let alone express an opinion. His vote is neutral—exactly like our lucky brother's."

She flew into a rage and started shouting. That was exactly what I had hoped for, but before the argument could escalate, her husband intervened and announced the results: "Two votes in favor, two against, and two neutral." With that, we were stuck. None of the votes could break the tie. So, based on the deadlock, we decided to discuss the method of participation instead.

Once again, Mother took the lead. This time, unlike before, her argument was so well-crafted that we all agreed with her, and the meeting came to an end. Her proposal was simple: the men would enroll in the *Independence Party*, while the women would join the *Stability Party*. This way, democracy would be upheld, and no matter which party gained power, our family's social standing would remain secure. With Mother's reasoning and our support behind her, our paths had been successfully divided. My sister and my mother would go their way, while my sister's husband and I would go ours.

The next morning, during office hours, we all left home together for the first time. My sister, who hadn't driven in a long time, took the wheel. The street leading to the *Independence Party* office was quiet, and she drove fast. We arrived early. My sister's husband and I got out of the car before reaching Revolution Square. We didn't want anyone to see that my sister had driven us to the office. The office was only 500 meters away, so we waited until she turned the corner before continuing on foot. Meanwhile, my mother and sister went off to enroll in the *Stability Party*.

The person in charge of the *Independence Party*'s registration recognized my sister's husband as soon as we entered. When he realized that we had come to enroll, he was overjoyed, and we encountered no issues while filling out the forms. Everything was completed in a flash, and within an hour, we both held membership cards for the *Independence Party*.

***

A seemingly unimportant incident ended up securing a strong position for us in the party. The story began two weeks before we became members when the government appointed a senior member of the *Independence Party* as mayor. At the time, we paid no attention to politics, and we wouldn't have even known about it if we hadn't become politically engaged under Mother's influence. After we joined the party, the new mayor signed a contract with my sister's husband to purchase certain equipment—equipment that, in reality, wasn't even necessary.

It was clear that the mayor was pleased with our membership. From then on, we no longer saw him only on holidays. Every morning, I received a list of requested products and, at the end of office hours, placed the delivery receipts on his desk. Without paying any attention to the type of goods, he would sign the payment order without hesitation.

Three months after we joined, my sister's husband and I attended the party's first public meeting. We were seated far from the platform. When the mayor entered through a door near us, everyone stood in his honor. I smiled proudly when he glanced around and saw me, though he showed no reaction. Still, I was happy—I assumed his indifference was simply due to the formality of the event. I took my seat again, but my sister's husband remained standing until the mayor walked to the front row and sat down. No sooner had my sister's husband taken his seat than a waiter approached us and invited us to move to the second row, directly behind the mayor. We both stood up and eagerly took our new seats. That day, we were thrilled to bits by our elevated status. We paid no mind to the jealous glances of other party members—at the time, we didn't even notice their envy. Later, however, we came to understand the fire that burned in their hearts when they saw the mayor extend his favor to us. Their resentment became evident through their disobedience and lack of cooperation— especially after my lucky brother had made a crucial misstep.

Of course, my sister's husband and I did not enjoy the same status. For example, while I was working tirelessly, he was effortlessly climbing the ranks. Before long, the mayor suggested appointing him as the party's treasurer due to his experience. However, the party leaders unanimously rejected the proposal. Instead, due to his limited experience, they appointed him as an official inspector—a significant position nonetheless. I suspected he would face challenges in his new role, as those who opposed him would not easily allow a newcomer to scrutinize their financial records.

However, he soon adapted to everything. Not only did he manage the accounts efficiently, but he also succeeded in satisfying everyone. Even the mayor himself mentioned this widespread satisfaction to me during one of our meetings when I went to collect the list of required equipment.

***

I didn't envy him at all. Eventually, I, too, received a promotion, though it took a little longer. Six months after the Public Congress of the Party—when the parliamentary elections began—I was suddenly appointed as the party's advertising agent by the mayor's order. Of course, I knew nothing about advertising, which worried me. Nevertheless, I took the appointment letter and went straight to my sister's husband to discuss it. He had gone home to escape the oppressive heat. I was immediately unsettled by the sight of his massive, furry body. He sat in front of me in short shorts, explaining the details of political advertising step by step. In the end, he reassured me that the party had many professional advertisers who would handle the work. All I had to do was give the orders, and they would take care of the rest.

That day, after seeing him in that state, I felt deeply sorry for my sister. I couldn't understand how she tolerated him, yet I had never once heard her complain.

The advertising campaign lasted a month. The first two weeks were spent preparing the propaganda, and for the next two weeks, we worked in the field. During the initial stage, I returned home around midnight. Only Mother was awake. I had never seen her sit on the balcony, gazing at the city before. I warned her that insomnia was harmful, but she simply replied that ever since Father's death, she had barely been able to sleep.

After those first two weeks, I stopped coming home at night altogether. We worked non-stop, plastering the city walls with posters of our candidates. In other words, anyone who stepped outside—no matter where—was greeted by the faces of our party's nominees. The mayor personally inspected our work and was so pleased that he called to thank me again.

Well, once, I had been the one burning the candle at both ends while my sister's husband got promotions. Now, many people were working tirelessly, and for once, it was all to my advantage.

The election was a great success. The *Independence Party* secured 382 out of 450 parliamentary seats, while the *Stability Party* suffered the worst defeat in its history. At least, that's what the newspapers reported. I swear to God, not only did I have no knowledge of the exact results, but even my mother and sister—who were *Stability Party* members—were completely unaware of them. In the end, the *Stability Party* won only 50 seats, while 18 seats went to independent candidates.

This victory was both a blessing and a curse. It was a blessing because both my sister's husband and I received promotions. I was appointed as the head of the mayor's office, and he was finally made the party's cashier. However, it was also a curse—because the moment the election results were announced, my mother and sister became our enemies.

Their hostility became apparent within the first few days, making it clear that my sister's husband and I could no longer stay in that house. We were about to pack up and leave when my mother and sister unexpectedly relented. But my sister's husband warned me that their change of heart was merely a facade. They haven't abandoned their resentment, he said. They've only hidden it.

Even though we had finally mastered the game, I couldn't shake an uneasy feeling. It was as if something invisible was looming over us, waiting to happen. I had butterflies in my stomach, an inexplicable sense of foreboding. I couldn't help but think we were climbing the ladder of success, only to eventually fall from the top.

One night, I even dreamed of that very fall. In my dream, we were plummeting, and my sister's husband was flailing his arms and legs in the air, desperately trying to save me. At the last moment, he grabbed the drawstrings of my pants, but instead of stopping the fall, they unraveled. As he drifted farther away, my pants got shorter and shorter. Fortunately, I woke up before I lost them entirely.

It was just a dream. In reality, everything was normal. We still had the world at our feet.

I hired a new employee to take over my duties in my sister's husband's companies. The new hire was middle-aged, perhaps a bit older. My sister had introduced her.

I took a day off and went to my sister's husband's offices to formally introduce her to the managers and explain her responsibilities in detail. She was expected to provide me with a daily report of her work every evening. However, on the first day, she failed to show up.

The following day, I called her and asked why she hadn't brought the report as expected. She responded in a self-righteous tone, saying that my sister had instructed her to report to her instead. Then, with a mocking tone, she asked, "Now tell me, who exactly should I be reporting to?"

Chapter 4

Although the opposing party had lost the election, the outcome ultimately worked in our favor. After the *Stability Party*'s defeat, they convened a global congress and dismissed all their leaders. The entire organizational structure was overhauled. Those who had previously held leadership positions were severely criticized and blamed for the party's failure. As a result, they were removed from their posts and demoted to ordinary members.

I first heard the news from the employee who had taken over my supervisory duties at the companies. My mother and sister, however, remained silent. Their lips were sealed—they still saw us as their enemies. The only information shared in our home was the announcement of the *Stability Party*'s new leadership appointments.

Despite the party's restructuring, my mother and sister managed to secure high-ranking positions. My mother was appointed as the representative of the Women's Association, while my sister became the head of the Advertising Office. She had chosen this position from among several options. It was clear she had ulterior motives—she had taken up the role hoping to exploit our expertise for her benefit.

However, the transition was not without obstacles. Whenever someone took on an important role, there were always those who had hoped for the position themselves and refused to accept the new appointments—just as it had happened in our party. My mother and sister's enemies saw our family's split allegiance between two rival parties as opportunism.

At first, rumors began to spread. The new employee, who reported daily tasks to my sister, informed her about the circulating gossip. My sister shared the news with us over dinner while we were eating soup. We all burst into laughter, but my mother warned, "Don't be so optimistic. This is just the beginning. Whoever started these rumors won't back down easily. We need to come up with an appropriate response."

My sister's husband and I continued eating our soup, indifferent to the discussion. Neither of us engaged in the argument, which only angered my mother further. Frustrated, she launched into a heated speech, accusing us of betrayal for disregarding the family's interests and failing to consider what was best for us.

My sister went even further. She called us spies and snapped, "If it weren't for you, we would have had a better status in the *Stability Party*. They don't trust us because we live with spies from the *Independence Party*."

Her husband burst into laughter. I laughed too, but to me, the delicious soup was more important than the argument. I let them have their debate. I didn't even bother to look up and see how they were glaring at each other.

My mother refrained from saying anything else in their presence, but as soon as I entered my bedroom, she stormed in without knocking. It was the first time she had ever done that. She was visibly upset and irritated.

I was naked, about to put on my pants, but before I could move, she ordered, "Sit the hell down. I have something to say."

She scolded me harshly, accusing me of being gluttonous and indifferent to our family's status. I refused to accept her accusations and replied, "This is a mess of your own making. Otherwise, I wouldn't have gotten involved in these games. You dragged me into this. And besides, how do you expect me to comment on something I know nothing about?"

She shot back, "You're lying to me. This is one of the tricks you learned from the *Independence Party*. You're keeping secrets."

I calmly responded, "You can believe whatever you want, but the truth is something else."

She let out a bitter laugh and said, "I'm not an important person in the party. If I were, you'd see just how much I could take."

Then, without waiting for my response, she slammed the door and stormed out of my bedroom. Of course, I had nothing to say. I was exhausted and had been waiting for her to leave so I could finally hit the sack.

Soon, the rumors spread among journalists. The first article about my sister appeared in Flag's weekly newspaper. It was a short letter, not particularly serious, and was even printed in the newspaper's comic strip section. My sister, however, reacted immediately, sending a sharp letter to the newspaper's chief editor. I was certain that someone had written it for her— perhaps one of the *Stability Party*'s leaders—because she never mentioned the article at home. It was clear that neither she nor my mother trusted us. The wording of the letter made it obvious that the thoughts expressed in it had never crossed her mind before.

In her response, she argued that their involvement in the party was purely due to their deep belief in democratic principles. She went on to elaborate on the supposed benefits of the *Stability Party*'s policies for women, claiming that she and my mother had carefully studied both parties' plans regarding women's rights. Yet, according to her, they had concluded that the *Independence Party* did not actually care about women's rights. At the end of the letter, she wrote that when they decided to join the *Stability Party*, they hadn't been influenced by my sister's husband or me, nor had they feared any threats from us.

Of course, none of what she had written was true. Even they knew that. The letter was nothing more than an attempt at revenge. And they had plenty of reasons to hold a grudge. Their latest grievance was obvious—it was because of our indifference at the dinner table, when I had chosen to focus on my oat soup rather than engage in their political discussion.

My sister's husband and I decided to carefully analyze the article away from my mother and sister. He called the Shell Hotel and booked a room. I wasn't sure why he had done that, but when we arrived and I took in the surrounding silence, I realized he had been right to choose such a secluded place.

My sister's response was so ambiguous that my sister's husband and I realized we could actually use it to our advantage within the *Independence Party*. I was ready to let the issue go, but my sister's husband, in party meetings, argued that we were so devoted to the *Independence Party* that we had even opposed our own family members.

Despite maintaining that stance, we decided to escalate our opposition. Our first move was to stop answering their phone calls. After work, instead of going home, we drove straight to the hotel. Before leaving, I instructed my secretary to tell them that we had left angrily if they called.

The twin room at the Shell Hotel was still reserved for us, but we started going there less frequently. We only used it when we wanted to work without any interference. Most of the time, we would sit in the hotel lobby, drink two cups of coffee, and leave without paying attention to anything else.

One evening, however, something unusual caught our attention—a large crowd gathered in front of a newsstand. I was curious and wanted to go buy a newspaper to see what the fuss was about, but my sister's husband stopped me.

"They're probably looking for your sister's nonsense comments," he said. "Let's forget about all this nonsense tonight."

Both of us laughed at those who eagerly followed those political commentaries, and instead, we wandered through the streets. By the end of the night, we found ourselves at a cozy and rather exclusive café.

I had never heard of it before that night. It turned out that the café was only for party members and their guests, and my sister's husband had a membership card. From the outside, nobody would have guessed it was a café—it was hidden in the middle of a vast open area, with no sign at the entrance.

The Shell Café—the café I had assumed was affiliated with the hotel—had a remarkably calm atmosphere. That night, for the first time, I openly praised my sister's husband for choosing such a quiet place. He explained that the Shell Café was more than just a café; it was a private club, and not just anyone could obtain a membership card. To become a member, one had to hold a privileged status in society or be introduced by a minister.

I immediately fell in love with the atmosphere. It gave me a sense of peace I had never experienced before. Right then and there, I decided that I would persuade the mayor to get me a membership card.

The only thing that bothered me slightly was the dim lighting. There were no overhead lights—or if there were, they had not been turned on. There were no windows to allow natural light inside. The only illumination came from dim lampshades placed on each table. The light was so weak that I could barely see my sister's husband, even though he was sitting less than half a meter away. As for the other guests, I couldn't make out anyone. That's why I had no idea who else was there that night. However, as we entered and left, I noticed that many tables remained empty.

We stayed at the café until shortly after midnight. According to the rules, we had to speak very quietly. My sister's husband mentioned this was part of the café's regulations, though I never saw any written rules on the dark walls, nor did anyone personally enforce them.

Because of this, I barely understood what he was saying. I have always struggled to hear people who speak softly. Even though I have my ears cleaned three times a year at the doctor's office, I still have difficulty catching words spoken in a hushed tone.

That night, I didn't bother trying too hard to follow what my sister's husband was saying. Eventually, we both got distracted and started talking nonsense. I found myself answering questions I hadn't even fully heard. I suspected he had the same problem because, at one point, I completely lost track of our conversation.

At one moment, my sister's husband reached for my wrist and held my watch under the table lamp. It was thirty-four minutes past midnight. We left the café and stepped outside into the cool night air.

He was in no condition to drive, so he handed his car keys to the café's operator and asked him to call a special taxi for us. We both sat in the back seat and started telling jokes. That night, I hadn't realized how close I had become to my sister's husband. We were so caught up in laughter that neither of us gave any thought to what we were saying.

As much as I enjoyed the calm, elegant, and mysterious atmosphere of the café—so different from the busy cafés I was used to—I found that I enjoyed being out in the open air even more.

Then, suddenly, the police stopped our taxi near the Shell Hotel. I frowned unhappily as the officer approached. He didn't say a word to us—he simply instructed the driver to follow him to the police station.

Given our background, fear gripped us immediately. My sister's husband and I were terrified because if we were arrested, our status would be in serious jeopardy. He was even more anxious than I was, as he didn't have enough money on him to resolve the issue if necessary.

I had always trusted my instincts to warn me of danger, but this time, I felt nothing. I was strangely calm inside. At first, I thought it was due to whatever I had eaten at the café.

Nervously, we followed the officer to the station. When the commander asked for our names and ordered an officer to check our records on the computer, our nerves were on edge. However, the officer behind the screen suddenly froze. His expression changed, and without a word, he stood up and walked over to his commander.

My sister's husband and I exchanged bewildered glances. We had no idea what was happening.

Then, the commander hurried toward us and began apologizing profusely, as if he had committed some grave mistake. We were stunned. At first, we thought they had mistaken us for someone else. But then he said something that made everything clear.

The commander admitted that the police department didn't know how to explain the situation to the mayor. He was deeply sorry for "insulting the chief of his office."

It was only then that we realized this was no mistake. They had deliberately arrested us. We were alert enough to ask what crime we had been charged of.

I simply asked to see my record. The officer printed a copy for me. Every detail was accurate, but the crime section was left completely blank. That confirmed my suspicion: someone had erased whatever charges had been there. The only question was—who had ordered the deletion of our alleged crimes from the system?

I didn't dwell on it too much. The important thing was that our records were clean, no matter who had intervened on our behalf.

The officer in charge scolded the patrol officer for arresting "two prominent officials." Meanwhile, our taxi had already left, so he personally drove us back to the hotel.

He was visibly shaken—especially when he realized we weren't going home but were instead heading back to the hotel. He seemed to suspect we were meeting someone there.

When we arrived, he didn't just drop us off in front of the building. He insisted on walking us toward the elevator, as if making sure we weren't up to something.

But as soon as the elevator doors opened, my sister's husband and I jumped inside. I quickly pressed the button to close the doors. The officer tried to step in, but my sister's husband placed his hand on the man's chest and held him back. Just as the doors slid shut, we escaped.

We were completely exhausted and slept like a rock until morning. Both of us arrived late to work, and it was only when we reached the mayor's office that we learned the prime minister had been shot the night before. That meant that while the country was in turmoil, we had been accused of indulging ourselves, oblivious to the crisis. I immediately called my sister's husband, but he had already heard the news—my sister had phoned him first. Before he could get a word in, she had unleashed a tirade of curses and accusations, demanding to know where the hell he had been the previous night. He told her the truth—that he had spent the entire night at the police station and had no idea why. But my sister was only interested in the bigger news—she informed him that the prime minister had been shot and was still unconscious.

That morning, as I reflected on everything that had happened at the café and afterward, I realized something: despite his rough appearance, my poor sister's husband was not such a bad person after all.

I went to the restroom and splashed cold water on my face. I made sure to compose myself, wiping away any signs of confusion or exhaustion from the previous night. When I returned to the office, the mayor had yet to arrive. Just as I sat down, my mother called. I didn't give her a chance to speak. Instead, I quickly told her about the erased records. Without hesitation, she hung up and went straight to the police station, demanding to see copies of both her own case and my sister's. Of course, she introduced herself as the mother of the head of the mayor's office and a member of the *Independence*

Party. The head of the police station wasted no time—he immediately printed copies of their records and handed them to her. Upon realizing that no crimes were listed in their files, my mother called me back, her voice filled with excitement. However, as soon as I told her that it was all thanks to the *Independence Party*, she hung up angrily—this time without even saying goodbye.

Chapter 5

My sister's husband was driving home from the company's headquarters on a rainy, dark evening when he was involved in an accident. He struck an oncoming motorcyclist on the left side of the street, throwing him onto the sidewalk. The motorcyclist died on the spot.

An hour after the accident, I received a call from the police station informing me of what had happened. I told my mother and sister that I was heading to my sister's husband's office and would be back late at night. They sensed something was wrong from my tone and grew worried, but I didn't reveal anything. I simply said that he was overwhelmed with work and had asked for my help.

Taking my sister's car, I drove to the secretary-general's office and called her from there. After staying for a short while, I returned home. However, my frequent comings and goings made my mother and sister suspicious. I had no choice but to tell them the truth.

Just as we were getting ready to go to the police station, the nine o'clock news broadcast covered the accident in shocking detail. The segment showed the poor Eastern

Othello and provided a full account of what had happened. At the end, they even aired footage of the young motorcyclist's lifeless body.

We were stunned. Why had the television station reported the incident so quickly?

My mother and sister were visibly shaken. They changed their mind after hearing the news and suddenly insisted that I go to the police station alone to get more information. Their reaction startled me—why had they both backed down so easily? No matter how much I pressed them, they refused to explain.

Reluctantly, I left home and made my way to the police station as quickly as possible. But when I arrived, I was informed that my sister's husband had already been taken into custody, and they refused to let me see him.

I pulled the guard officer aside and asked to speak with him privately, but he hesitated, unwilling to talk in secret in front of others. Instead, he led me into a room where several other officers were present and explained the situation in full detail.

The victim, it turned out, was the adopted son of a senior municipal officer and a member of the *Stability Party.*

When I heard this, I shuddered with fear. To be honest, I immediately thought that my sister's husband was doomed. I barely processed what the officer was saying—my mind was too busy racing through the consequences of this disaster.

The officer seemed to notice my lack of attention. As I prepared to leave, he added, "Given the victim's status within the *Stability Party*, if we had tried to cover anything up, we would have faced serious problems. Since the police do not interfere in political matters, we wanted the public to hear the truth exactly as it happened."

I walked out of the police station, hesitant to return home. But it was still raining, and I couldn't stay outside. At the same time, I feared that in this dark, stormy weather, I might end up in an accident just like my sister's husband. Knowing my luck, I'd probably have a head-on collision with the secretary-general of the party.

With no other choice, I reluctantly returned home and relayed everything I had learned to my sister. She recognized the victim immediately and explained that his father was the deputy secretary-general of the *Stability Party*. His mother, after divorcing him, had remarried a senior officer. As a result, the victim had two fathers—his biological father and his influential stepfather. He had maintained good relationships with both of them.

With his father's influence, he had been appointed as the head of the Youth Organization within the *Stability Party*.

My mother, who had been listening to our conversation, began moaning loudly. I dared to glance at her seriously, but instead of reacting, she began speaking. She recounted several times she had met the young man at general party meetings and spoke highly of him. She deeply regretted his death, lamenting that a young man with such a promising future had been lost.

Then, with a grave expression, she declared, "His death will bring irreparable damage to the party."

I hadn't expected them to give up so easily. Both my mother and sister declared that they had no intention of lifting a finger for Othello. My sister went even further, insisting that we must not mix family matters with party responsibilities. It was the *Independence Party*'s duty to take care of its prominent members—not theirs.

Furious, I accused them of betrayal in a heated speech. But instead of responding, they dismissed me entirely, mocking me as they got dressed and left the house together. I knew exactly where they were going—to meet the deputy secretary-general.

Determined, I grabbed my mother's car and sped toward the mayor's house. But when I arrived, his wife informed me that he had gone to the prime minister's office.

By that point, I could barely drive in the worsening weather. In addition to my hearing loss, I also struggle with vision problems. If the conditions outside became even slightly unusual, I would lose control. And besides, I had already been running around the city all night.

Reluctantly, I left the car in the mayor's garage and took a taxi instead. I ordered the driver to take me straight to the prime minister's palace.

Near the entrance, I told the guard to let the driver wait. He shook his head in refusal. Without hesitation, I pulled out my identification card. At the sight of it, the guard immediately relented.

I rushed into the prime minister's office, where I found the manager—a man I knew well. As soon as I explained the situation, he quickly alerted the mayor, who came rushing out.

I told him everything: the details of my sister's husband's accident and, most crucially, the identity of the victim. The mayor grabbed my hand and led me straight to the prime minister's room.

Both of them were deeply alarmed. Without hesitation, they contacted the Central Committee and scheduled an emergency meeting for the following morning at ten o'clock. The prime minister instructed me to attend the meeting and present a full report on the incident. However, both he and the mayor made one thing clear—I was not to inform my mother or sister about the meeting.

I obeyed without question. Even if they hadn't told me to keep it secret, I would never have let them get wind of it.

Despite my worries, I couldn't help but feel a surge of satisfaction. I had managed to communicate directly with the prime minister and other high-ranking government officials. However, the situation itself deeply troubled me. In my opinion, a minor accident was now spiraling into an excuse for all-out war between the two parties. A war that no one could predict the outcome of. And that was why I couldn't forgive my mother and sister. They had abandoned us in our time of need—and, worse, they had been to the victim's father's house to add fuel to the fire.

I was certain that my mother and sister had had significant discussions with the leaders of the *Stability Party*. They said nothing when they returned home, pretending to be exhausted and going straight to bed. The way they acted—both following the same routine, as if they had rehearsed it—only confirmed my suspicions. Mother wasn't even surprised when she noticed that her car wasn't in the yard. But the most striking thing of all was my sister's complete indifference. Despite the fact that her husband was in serious trouble, she showed no concern, no anxiety— nothing. She remained as cool as a cucumber.

I followed her to her bedroom, but just as I was about to enter, she stretched out her hand, stopping me. Yawning, she said casually, "This is just the beginning. We'll still be alive tomorrow. They're not going to hang him tonight."

I went to speak with my mother, but she pretended to be asleep and ignored me.

I couldn't close my eyes all night. Early in the morning, before they woke up, I got up, went to the bathroom, shaved, got dressed, and sat in the living room, waiting for them. At exactly eight o'clock, both of them emerged from their rooms—moving in perfect sync, as if they were actors following a director's orders. At that moment, I became absolutely certain. They didn't care about my sister's husband.

The war between the two parties had escalated within our own home. That morning, my sister took a shower, just as I had, and then sat in front of her dressing table for an entire hour, applying heavy makeup as if she were preparing for a wedding. Mother hovered nearby, assisting her with the care and devotion of a woman getting her daughter ready to meet suitors. Once they were finished, I approached my sister, intending to speak with her, but before I could say a word, the doorbell rang. I rushed to answer it, but my sister quickly pressed the FF button, unlocking the door before I could react. Two young men stepped inside together. I asked them why they had come, but they ignored me and walked straight to my sister. She shook hands with both of them and led them into the living room. I followed, uneasy. One of the men opened his bag and pulled out a camera and a tape recorder. That was when I realized—she had started a dangerous game. I stepped in front of them and shouted, accusing her of betraying her husband. My sister met my gaze, unfazed, then subtly gestured toward our mother. Despite her age, Mother had also dressed up to the nines that morning. Without hesitation, she grabbed my arm and dragged me out of the living room. Furious, I called for a taxi. It arrived quickly. I was already running late, and the Central Committee meeting was about to start. I ordered the driver to take me straight to party headquarters.

By the time I arrived, the meeting had already been underway for ten minutes. I apologized and informed them about my sister's interview. Everyone was immediately concerned. I assured them that I had done everything in my power to stop her from speaking, but it was clear that the *Stability Party* had carefully orchestrated this move. They began discussing the situation, but I could barely follow their words. I sat in silence, simply watching the people around me.

The meeting lasted an hour and a half. At the end, the prime minister gave me direct instructions—I was to remain in contact with his office 24/7 and not take any action without his explicit permission. Hearing that, I couldn't help but feel a surge of pride. Despite the chaos, I felt an odd sense of satisfaction. My sister might not have been entirely wrong after all. Perhaps the leaders of the *Stability Party* or those around them had treated her with such importance that she now believed she held true power. And yet, I recognized that I, too, was experiencing that same intoxicating feeling.

That evening, The *Evening Newspaper* published my sister's interview, complete with a full-face photograph of her. I was afraid to read what she had said. One thing was certain—my sister's husband was doomed. She had claimed that her husband already knew the victim. She alleged that she had frequently visited the victim's house for party-related matters and that her husband had always objected to those meetings taking place there. She even stated that he had once argued with the victim. Her words were framed in a way that sounded as if the accident had been a premeditated assassination.

***

The *Stability Party* seized the moment, calling upon all its members and supporters—especially the youth—to participate in a massive protest march. The party's bulletin, The *Stability Newspaper*, announced the march's planned route:

- It would begin at the party's office,

- Pass by the headquarters of my sister's husband's company,

- Reach the small square near our home,

- And conclude with the reading of their resolution.

My first priority was ensuring the safety of the company's employees. I ordered them not to come to work that day to avoid any potential danger. Next, I called the prime minister's office to consult with him. He informed me that he had already issued orders—the members of our party were to gather on both sides of the street and beat pots with ladles to drown out the voices of the protesters. I rushed to the party's office. The atmosphere was anything but normal. People hurried in and out, everyone seemingly occupied with urgent matters. The deputy secretary-general pulled me aside and instructed me to stay home and report anything I overheard from my mother and sister. I assured him that both of them had become reticent— that their lips were sealed.

However, the *Stability Party* seemed to have been spying on us. Before news of our plan to use ladles and pots had even reached our own members, they had already found out. They had decided to twist the act into something else—claiming it was a blatant display of suppression.

And they were preparing to fight back.

***

On the day of the march, each member and supporter of the *Stability Party* carried either a trumpet or a drum. However, the trumpets had corks stuffed into their holes, and the drums lacked drumheads. They marched with solemn dignity, playing their instruments silently, walking the designated route without making a sound.

Meanwhile, we, the members of the *Independence Party*, took a different approach. We created such an uproar with the clatter of pots and ladles that midway through, we had to stuff cotton balls in our ears to protect our eardrums from the very noise we refused to silence. I had placed a large pot on a stool near the curb and was striking it furiously with a steel ladle.

Despite the deafening racket, the *Stability Party* marchers remained unbothered. They calmly followed their predetermined path, showing no reaction. But in a sudden, impromptu decision, the deputy secretary-general—the victim's father—climbed onto a chair to read the resolution. Instead of speaking, he merely mimed, as if to demonstrate that his voice had been stifled. His supporters responded with silent applause before peacefully dispersing.

The anti-government newspapers sensationalized the march, while the pro-government papers mocked it, deploying every humorist at their disposal. One particularly sharp remark claimed that the voices of the protesters had started from nowhere and disappeared into oblivion.

This enraged my mother and sister, who had been at the front of the march. Firstly, they both lashed out at me, accusing me of betraying my own family by belonging to such an "infamous and murderous" party. I calmly reminded them that if a murder had indeed taken place, we had to acknowledge that a member of our own family had committed it.

Secondly, they seemed to have entirely forgotten why we had joined political parties in the first place. But given how things had unfolded, their original reasoning was now lost to them.

***

The following day, The *Independence Newspaper*, a publication affiliated with our party, printed an article that turned my home life into a nightmare. The piece exposed details about my sister's past, referencing statements from employees at various private companies and hospitals where she had worked before getting married. Furious, she threw me out of the house. Not that I minded—I had no desire to stay there anymore. Seizing the opportunity, I decided to take advantage of my connections. I called the mayor and told him about my situation. He immediately contacted the Shell Café, and within minutes, they issued me a temporary membership card. That night, I stayed at the café alone until midnight. It was a refreshing change—no poor Othello droning on, no unwanted company. For the first time, I savored the pleasure of solitude, of being free from intrusions. By the time midnight arrived, my mind felt so unburdened that I had momentarily forgotten all the turmoil. When I finally stood up to leave, a waiter escorted me to the front door, where a special taxi—called by the café itself—was waiting to take me to the Shell Hotel.

They had prepared a well-equipped room for me. Unlike the night I had previously spent there with my sister's husband, I couldn't sleep at all. Even the hotel manager's secretary brought me some sleeping pills, but they couldn't help.

It wasn't until early in the morning that exhaustion finally overtook me, and I slept until eleven o'clock. When I woke up, the hotel manager was standing over me. "We've been calling your room for hours," he said. "The mayor's office has been trying to reach you."

I rubbed my eyes, still groggy. "I must have slept through it. I didn't hear the phone ringing."

The hotel manager shook his head. "The mayor has ordered that you are not to leave the room or take any phone calls."

I asked him, "Why?"

He replied that he didn't know anything—he was simply relaying the mayor's message. With that, he left.

My body went limp with fear. I had no idea what to do. I paced around the room, circling it several times, feeling as though I was on the verge of losing my mind.

Finally, I called the hotel manager and told him to come to my room immediately. My room was on the fifteenth floor, the highest floor in the hotel. Above it was only the Snake Restaurant.

The manager arrived in a hurry. I told him I was losing my grip. He reassured me, saying that he had been friends with the mayor for thirty years, had been a loyal member of the *Independence Party* since its founding, and would do everything in his power to assist me.

Without wasting time, he called someone to bring me a multiwave radio and both the morning and evening newspapers.

As soon as I saw the newspapers, my heart pounded. Both parties were playing a dangerous game—and I had become their pawn. My photo was printed on the front page. The bold headlines screamed that I had disappeared, warning of sinister conspiracies against me, the trusted friend of my sister's husband. One newspaper even accused my mother and sister of kidnapping me, claiming that, with the help of secret agents, they had abducted a loyal member of the *Independence Party* simply because I had protested against their heinous acts.

In an interview, the mayor himself had stated that my last phone call with him had been suddenly cut off. To make things even worse, they had published a photograph of my empty chair—my missing presence turned into a symbol. No wonder I was terrified. I felt sick in such a situation, my worry growing with every passing moment. I carefully read all the news and reports, trying to grasp the full scope of the narrative being spun around me. The articles were all identical—it was clear they had come from a single source. I turned on the radio. Every station played soft, soothing music. It was as if the world had suddenly found peace with my disappearance—or perhaps the entire world had conspired to calm me down.

I called the hotel manager again. "This is driving me crazy. I swear, I'll throw myself out of the window into the courtyard right now."

He rushed to my room, his face tense. Without a word, he yanked the curtains aside, letting light flood the space. Then, he grabbed the phone from the table and made a call. I didn't listen. I barely understood anything anymore. A few minutes later, a young woman entered, carrying a beautiful guitar. With his back to me, the hotel manager whispered something to her before quietly leaving the room.

The musician sat in front of my bed and began playing a song I knew well—one composed by a Mexican musician. But instead of simply listening and enjoying it, I found myself wondering... How did they know I liked this song? She played until the final note. Then, she repeated the melody. Every now and then, she lifted her gaze from the guitar and glanced at me. I remained motionless, staring at her, dazed, until I suddenly began trembling. The repetition of the melodies became unbearable. Then, abruptly, she stopped playing. She smiled at me. I leaned back against the pillows and took a deep breath, relieved. I was about to tell her to leave when she started playing another piece—one that I liked even more. Then, she sang, her soft, delicate voice making it impossible for me to think of objecting. Her voice was so gentle that I closed my eyes and simply listened. She sang in Spanish, and her voice flowed effortlessly, gliding through the air. For a brief moment, I forgot my troubles. I forgot everything. I just wanted the music—and her voice—to last forever.

I don't know how much time passed before someone knocked on the door. I opened my eyes. The hotel manager entered, carrying a tray of food—without asking permission. The meal was only for one person.

I asked him to bring something for the musician as well, but he shook his head and said, "After you have lunch, a new musician will be at your service." I didn't want another musician. But she seemed tired. She didn't wait for an invitation to stay. As soon as she heard what the manager said, she picked up her guitar and left.

I ate my lunch quickly, placed the tray on the table, and lay down on the bed. Closing my eyes, I replayed the events of the past few days in my mind.

I was angry—mostly at my sister and mother, but especially at my sister, who seemed to be betraying her poor husband. However, I had to admit that the mayor had handled the situation well. I hoped that his actions would force my mother and sister to think rationally and abandon their schemes against the unfortunate Othello.

At the same time, I couldn't shake the fear that the mayor, like my mother and sister, was more concerned with the party's interests than with my well-being. That realization unsettled me, but it was unavoidable. I had no choice but to surrender to events as they unfolded. Still, I reassured myself that the mayor had no ill intentions—he simply wanted to restrain my sister.

An hour after lunch, another musician entered my room. I opened my eyes at the sound of the door and, for a moment, I thought she was the same musician as before. She looked almost identical—the same height, the same face. The only difference was that her nose was slightly narrower. When she started playing, I noticed that her fingers were even more delicate. She played a few songs—all ones I loved. But this time, instead of soothing me, the music unsettled me.

***

After reading the news reports, I realized that my situation had caused a public uproar. Yet, I had turned a deaf ear to all of it. The chaos benefited the mayor more than it did me. My circumstances at the hotel had made me increasingly suspicious. I started questioning everything—was this really a hotel? Was that man really its manager? I was no longer paying attention to the music. Then, panic set in. The musician's voice was exactly like the previous musician's—as if they shared the same vocal cords. I walked to the window, ignoring her. Outside, I saw the hotel's courtyard. The water in the pool was a vibrant blue, and young and old guests alike were swimming, bouncing up and down in the water, carefree. That sight reassured me. This was a real hotel. I returned to my place. The musician was still playing softly, her voice gentle and calming. I lay down, closed my eyes—Then, suddenly, she struck a note harshly, and the song ended abruptly. I opened my eyes just in time to see her standing up and leaving with her guitar. I felt relieved. Finally, I would be alone in my room, free from strangers, free to lie on my bed in peace. I no longer needed to wear formal clothes in the presence of others. I took off my coat and pants, hanging them neatly in the closet. Then, I removed my shirt and hung it beside them. Wearing only my shorts and underwear, I jumped onto the bed. But just as I got comfortable—Knock, knock. Before I could even react, the hotel manager entered the room. I hurried toward the closet to get dressed, but before I could, he grabbed my arm and led me back to the bed. He sat down on the couch where I had been sitting minutes earlier.

Then, he asked casually, "Do you need anything?"

I answered quickly, "No. I don't need anything."

He raised an eyebrow. "Why are you in such a hurry to answer?"

"Because I'm afraid you'll send more people like those two musicians," I said. "They unsettled me more than they calmed me."

The hotel manager tilted his head. "What did they do?"

"Nothing." I sighed. "Firstly, they're identical. Secondly, their voices are exactly the same. And thirdly, they played music I already had in my mind—without even asking me what I liked."

The manager smiled slightly. "You're worrying for no reason. Firstly, they're identical twins. Secondly, we were instructed to play only those songs for you."

I stared at him, my mind racing. He looked at me with a calm, almost gentle expression. His tranquility unnerved me—I felt lost, unsure of how to respond. Who had told him that I liked those songs? Who had given the orders? Why had I been sent to this hotel? I cursed the day my sister met that scumbag Othello— whether it was on the street, at the company, or anywhere else. He had dragged us into this disaster.

I asked the hotel manager, "Am I ever allowed to swim in the yard pool?"

He raised an eyebrow. "Do you want to swim only in the yard pool?"

"No," I replied. "It doesn't make a difference if there's another pool."

He nodded. "Tomorrow, the rooftop pool will be ready for you."

I hesitated. "Up on the roof?"

"Yes. The rooftop swimming pool is behind the Snake Restaurant. It's reserved exclusively for special guests. Anything else?"

"No, thanks. That's all for now."

The hotel manager stood up, bowed slightly, and left the room. I lay back down on the bed and quickly drifted off to sleep. When I woke up, the room was completely dark. I reached for the radio and switched to the local stations, hoping for some useful information, but they had nothing relevant to say. I decided to switch to foreign stations, but there was still half an hour before their first news programs began. I tuned in to a station and placed the radio beside my head. When the news started, I jolted upright in fear and rushed to the window. The broadcaster announced my disappearance in the news summary, and in the commentary section, they were about to air an interview with my sister. I stood frozen, waiting for the news to end—but it dragged on endlessly. It felt like hours before I finally heard my sister's ominous voice—the very voice I had been trying to forget. She blamed the *Independence Party* for my disappearance, accusing them of orchestrating the entire situation to distract from the murder and cover it up. She vowed to uncover the truth and expose the party's deception.

The interviewer then asked her, "Did you have any personal conflicts with your brother?"

She twisted everything. She claimed that her husband had been the one trying to create division between us, but that she and I had always ignored such conspiracies. Immediately after, the radio station aired an interview with the mayor. Hearing his voice steadied me.

He stated firmly that the disappearance of his office's head was a serious matter and that the police were monitoring the situation closely. He accused the *Stability Party* of kidnapping and, in conclusion, announced that the *Independence Party* would be holding a mass protest the following day.

The demonstration was meant to denounce the conspiracies and marches organized by the *Stability Party* and to show loyalty to two key individuals—one accused of murder and the other, abducted.

The protest's route was deliberate: it would begin at the municipal building and end at the home I shared with my mother and sister.

And then, the mayor's final words hit me like a blow.

"We have chosen this path specifically to send a message to the traitorous mother and sister of the head of my office—who have betrayed him."

Things were getting worse—more serious by the minute. If this continued, with both parties stubbornly opposing each other, I felt I would go mad, trapped in that hotel.

I had to do something to save myself. I decided to call the hotel manager and ask him to arrange a meeting with the mayor. I was still thinking about it when suddenly, someone knocked on the door. Before I could even stand up, the hotel manager entered, carrying a package in his hands. Without a word, he placed it on the bed and opened it, pulling out a navy-blue suit. Then, he began dressing me in it. He handed me a sky-blue shirt and a red tie. I had no idea why he was dressing me up or where I was supposed to go. I was so confused that I couldn't even ask. The manager worked quickly, as if he was already late and didn't want to waste another second. I had completely surrendered to him, letting him prepare me without protest.

Once he finished, he stepped forward, and I followed. We left the room. The hallway was dark and silent, not a single person in sight except the two of us. I longed to escape that suffocating atmosphere, but when the elevator doors opened, I was startled to see the hotel manager enter before me. The elevator was empty. The manager pressed B2. Panic gripped me. Why underground? Where is he taking me? Before I could say anything, the doors slid shut, and the elevator began descending—slowly. I didn't dare speak. I just counted the seconds until the doors would open so I could throw myself out. When they finally did, I was met with an unexpected sight—a white car parked just outside the elevator doors, its driver waiting beside it. The driver reached into his pocket and pulled out a card. I recognized it immediately. It was the same kind my sister's husband had—the exclusive membership card for the Shell Café. A wave of relief washed over me. But then, I noticed something strange. My sister's husband's card had been green. The card they gave me was red. The hotel manager offered no explanation. He simply opened the car door with a small gesture, and without questioning it, I got in. The driver remained silent. He didn't say a single word as he pulled away.

When we arrived at the café, they took my card and didn't return it. I turned to the officer at the door. "I need my card. It should stay with me." The officer replied flatly, "This card is temporary. It's only valid for one night."

At that moment, I understood why my card had been a different color. My sister's husband's green card was permanent.

I stayed in the café until almost morning. It felt like the best place in the world. No one disturbed me. Even if someone sat beside you, you were supposed to speak so quietly that your voice couldn't be heard, just as you couldn't hear anyone else's. And I had no companion. For the first time in what felt like forever, I was completely at peace. I didn't want to leave. But as dawn approached, a waiter came to inform me that my driver was waiting at the front door. Reluctantly, I stood up and made my way out. It was the same driver as before. I moved toward the front seat, but the driver motioned for me to sit in the back. Again, he said nothing. No questions. No hints. I told myself, Maybe they've already given him the address. I must be going home now. First, I'll wake my sister up and beat her to death. Then, I'll separate my financial accounts from my mother's.

I had no idea where the driver was taking me. Half-asleep, I drifted in and out of a nap. When I finally woke up, I saw the Shell Hotel building in the distance. A wave of fear washed over me. My body began trembling. He's taking me back to that damn room. Panic surged through me. I wanted to fling the car door open and jump out, but the vehicle was moving too fast. I decided to make a run for it as soon as the car stopped in the parking lot. But instead of stopping there, the driver sped into the basement, pulling up beside the elevator.

The hotel manager was already there, waiting for me. As I reached for the door handle, he stepped forward and opened it himself. Then, without a word, he grabbed my arm. I struggled to get out of the car, my fear obvious. I glanced at his face, searching for any sign of what was to come. But he remained calm—unshaken. I berated myself. Did you really think you could escape like this?

Without resistance, I let him lead me into the elevator. We ascended. I was back in that room again. The hotel manager removed my clothes and placed me on the bed to rest.

I woke up at half past eleven the next morning, still dazed and disoriented. The first thing I noticed was a stack of newspapers on the tea table. I grabbed them immediately. There, on the front page of The *Independence Newspaper*, was a large photograph of my mother and sister. They were banging on pots with ladles. Beneath the image, the caption read: "Members of the *Stability Party* disrupt the *Independence Party*'s silent march." I stared at the photo carefully. The pots and ladles they were holding weren't the ones I had used. I muttered to myself, If the *Stability Party* hadn't bought them those pots and ladles, their household items would have been destroyed by now.

The report detailed that our party had mirrored the *Stability Party*'s tactics—marching in silence with trumpets whose holes had been sealed and drums without drumheads. The only real noise had come from the banging of pots and ladles of protestors. It was as if they were leading the march. Just like that day when I had stood in front of the house. I regretted not being there. If I had participated, they might have given me a trumpet too. I imagined it—arriving at the front door, standing before my sister, playing the trumpet, stamping my feet on the ground. That would've been the perfect way to settle accounts with that ungrateful woman.

The newspapers reported that my sister had remained firm in her position, openly siding with the *Stability Party* over her own husband. That night, foreign radio stations announced the impending trial of my sister's husband. Poor Othello. What must he be feeling? Maybe he thought I was ungrateful for not visiting him. Or maybe he already knew the truth—that I had been kidnapped.

Chapter 6

The trial of my sister's husband had begun. I learned about it through the press. Radio and television paid little attention to the case. They only broadcast brief court updates, including a segment of the trial, particularly Othello's defense. Ever since the hotel manager had informed me that the first court session would take place the following day, I had ants in my pants. The room felt like a prison cell. I imagined that my sister's husband was experiencing the same suffocating confinement in his actual cell. He was probably cursing everyone—even me.

The next morning, they brought me the newspapers. I had just finished breakfast and had nothing else to do. So, I lay on the bed and began reading. Othello's statement was exactly what I had read in interviews with his defense lawyer—a law professor and a prominent member of the *Independence Party*. But what affected me the most wasn't his words. It was his picture. He had lost so much weight—his once full face now gaunt and hollow. He looked hideous. In my opinion, even my sister wouldn't be able to look at him now.

In court, my sister's husband argued that the accident had been caused by the heavy rain and the slippery asphalt. He insisted that not only had he had no intention of harming anyone, but—contrary to his wife's statement—he had never even met the victim. There was no prior enmity between them. His defense was solid. He pointed out that the victim had been wearing a black raincoat and a helmet—making it impossible to recognize who was approaching. He claimed the murder charge was nothing more than a conspiracy by the *Stability Party*—just like the kidnapping of his wife's brother because of being friendly with him. He even stated that he wasn't sure if I was still alive. Reading that made me oddly happy. My abduction was now public knowledge. I skimmed through the rest of the court reports. Nothing else mattered anymore—I had been acquitted in the public eye. I could now go anywhere with peace of mind. No one would accuse me of being ungrateful anymore. I silently praised the intelligence and strategy of the mayor and the hotel manager. When I finished reading, I tossed the newspaper aside, stood up, and walked to the bathroom—snapping my fingers as I went.

After bathing, I called the front desk and ordered lunch. This time, the hotel manager himself dined with me. It was only then that I realized I had never paid much attention to him before. He sat across from me, eating slowly. Every time he lifted his spoon, he lowered his head slightly—giving me the perfect opportunity to study his face. He was old. The skin under his eyes was puffed up, like two heavy bags hanging from his face. Even though he was polite and well-mannered, I did not like his appearance. Not at all.

As soon as the manager entered my room, he mentioned that he liked to listen to music while eating. Without hesitation, he called the receptionist and asked them to send the musicians up. We had barely started eating when one of the twins arrived—I couldn't tell whether it was the first one or the second one—and began playing the manager's favorite music. It was an Indian song. I didn't like Indian songs at all, but out of respect for a polite man like the manager, I forced myself to listen calmly. The manager took his time with his meal, showing no hurry to finish. The food was enough for several people. If he hadn't been there, I would have asked the musician to set aside his guitar and join me. But I had learned by now that the waiters and musicians were merely part of the hotel's service. And so, I played along—acting with the air of someone accustomed to luxury.

***

The trial of my sister's husband lasted three days. Each morning, I pored over the newspapers, following every detail of the proceedings. By the end of those three days, my room looked more like a garbage dump than a hotel suite—piles of crumpled newspapers scattered everywhere.

At night, I would slip away to the Shell Café, staying there until morning. Each night, they issued me a temporary card. Finally, on the last night, I turned to the hotel manager and asked for a permanent one. He shook his head. "The number of tables at the Shell Café is limited. Permanent cards are not issued. But I might be able to get you your sister's husband's card."

I just stared at him. I wanted to say something, but I held my tongue. It wasn't difficult to read between the lines—he was implying that my sister's husband was as good as dead.

***

The following night, the mayor came to visit me for the first time. Together, we went to the Shell Café. He, of course, had a permanent card. I tried to speak to him on the way, but the hotel manager shot me a warning look, motioning for me to stay quiet. I had no choice but to wait for the right moment. Sensing my impatience, the mayor tapped me on the shoulder and offered a reassuring smile. It seemed he already knew what I wanted to say.

Inside the Shell Café, he didn't sit across from me. Instead, he angled his chair so that he was right beside me, then leaned in close and asked, "What did you want to say?"

I answered immediately, "I don't want to stay in the hotel anymore. It's driving me up the wall. My nerves are frayed. I want to go home as soon as possible."

He exhaled slowly. "It's better if you stay in the hotel for a few more days—at least until your sister's husband's case is finalized."

Then, with complete certainty, he added, "His fate is clear. He'll be executed."

I swallowed hard, but he continued, "You should keep a low profile. You might still be arrested for deceiving the police."

I hesitated, then asked, "So when can I return home?"

He shook his head. "That house is no longer a safe place for you. We have to figure something out."

I said nothing. Unlike the mayor, I knew my mother and sister very well. With a few tricks, I could manipulate them into letting me stay. But my thoughts drifted to the house itself. Everything would change once my sister's husband was executed. If he died, my sister would inherit all of his wealth. It had nothing to do with me. And if she was furious with me? If she kicked me out? I wouldn't last a single night. With the game the *Independence Party* had started, she would be up in arms. After thinking it over, I made my decision. I would win my sister over. But not yet. I would wait— wait to see what the mayor planned for my future outside the house. And once I was secure again... I would reunite with my sister. And together, we would expose the tricks of the *Independence Party*—at the right moment.

That night, the mayor told me that he had a close relationship with the judge presiding over my sister's husband's case. He hinted that the judge would likely not rule in Othello's favor and would probably sentence him to execution for murder. A week later, just as the mayor had predicted, the judge sentenced him to death.

The verdict was confirmed immediately, and he was hanged the following day. When I saw his final photograph in the newspaper, my heart went out to him. Poor Othello! He had been the only casualty of a conspiracy that spared everyone except him. In the last days of his life, he had come to resemble my father—his body thinner, his posture shrunken. The photo showed him standing on a stool, staring at the noose in front of him.

I desperately wanted to know what he had been thinking in those final minutes. What were his last thoughts about me? About my sister? About my mother? Now, not only did I not know, but nobody ever would. The day after my sister's husband was executed, no one came to see me. A thin, young man brought me my meals. I called the hotel manager, but no one answered the phone. That evening, when the young man returned with dinner, I asked about the manager again. In a quiet, feeble voice, he simply replied, "I have no idea." What could that fool possibly know? Then, suddenly, a thought struck me—I need to escape. Now that they were playing with my life, it was time for me to take matters into my own hands. Maybe I could still slip away, before it was too late.

My sister had sacrificed her husband for wealth and power—or at least, she pretended that she was defending her beliefs and the *Stability Party*. What if they were planning the same fate for me? What if they were ready to give me up just as easily? If I was nothing more than a pawn in their political game, I would end up in a grave.

I turned the doorknob. Locked. My stomach dropped. They had anticipated my thoughts before I even acted. I hadn't heard the door being locked, but now that I knew it was, my whole body trembled with fear. I was trapped. Completely surrounded. I knew then that no one was coming for me. No one would take me to the Shell Café like they had on previous nights. I had guessed correctly. No one came. Not even to bring me dinner. I paced the room restlessly, my mind racing, replaying every possible escape plan. From the window, I watched cars pulling into the parking lot, others driving out. I imagined their occupants, returning from the Shell Café, carrying on with their lives— while everyone ignored me. For hours, I walked back and forth, plotting.

By 3 a.m., I had made my decision. I would stand behind the door, wait for the waiter to bring breakfast, and the moment he stepped inside—I would attack. A few punches would be enough to knock him out. Then, I would steal his uniform and walk out of the room unnoticed. Once free, I would go straight to my sister, tell her everything, and urge her and our mother to expose the truth—with the help of their connections in the *Stability Party*.

All of a sudden, before I could put my plan into action—BANG. The door slammed open with force. I barely had time to react before three figures entered the room— The mayor. The hotel manager. And a middle-aged man I didn't recognize. I staggered backward until my back hit the wall. I was bracing myself, expecting more people to enter—But the mayor stepped forward, smiled warmly, and kissed me on the cheek. "Dear friend, everything is over," he said kindly. "You can go home now. But first, you need to answer a few questions from these gentlemen."

Strangely, no one actually asked me anything. The stranger didn't even look at me. Then, without another word, the hotel manager left the room, and we followed him.

From the hotel, we drove straight to police headquarters. They seated me in a chair, and the middle-aged man—the police chief, I soon realized—greeted me warmly. But something was off. A camera was recording everything. Why were they filming a greeting? I felt relieved that I was no longer in danger, but my nerves were shot. I wanted to get up and leave, but they wouldn't stop greeting me. The endless formalities were driving me insane. Finally, I couldn't take it anymore. Using the excuse of needing to go to the bathroom, I stood up—without asking permission—and walked toward the door with the toilet sign. The mayor immediately stepped toward me.

Frustrated, I turned to him and asked, "Why won't that man stop greeting me?" He smiled, reached out, and gently caressed my cheek. Then, in a reassuring voice, he said, "Don't worry. It's for your own good." I was angry with the mayor, too, but there was nothing I could do— except go to the lavatory and sit behind the closed door, finally at peace. I stayed there long enough for them to start worrying. Soon, they began knocking on the door. To put their minds at ease, I made a few deliberate ohm ohm sounds. When I finally came out, I was met with videographers, cameras in hand, ready to capture my exit.

By six o'clock in the morning, inside the police headquarters, I finally understood what had happened.

The radio news revealed everything. They had fabricated a dramatic rescue story, claiming that the night before, I had been saved from the clutches of *Stability Party* operatives who had been hiding me— with the help of my sister and mother. The radio broadcast stirred up an incredible amount of public outrage.

I muttered to myself, "TV will definitely air the footage tonight. But why hasn't anyone questioned me about it? Which video are they even planning to show?"

Every time they had filmed me, I had either been greeting the commander or walking out of the restroom. At seven o'clock in the morning, my sister and mother arrived at police headquarters. Unfortunately, they caused a huge scene. Though I was in another room, eating breakfast, I could hear them loud and clear. The mayor was also present, but I barely noticed him. On the radio, I heard a live interview with the police commander. "For security reasons," he announced, "we cannot allow the mother and sister of the head of the mayor's office to meet him." Then, he dropped another bombshell. He claimed that two individuals who had been holding the kidnapped man in the basement of a garden on the outskirts of the city had been arrested.

With the permission of the prosecutor, he explained, the police had tracked the kidnappers through the phone records of the mother and sister of the head of the mayor's office—leading them to their breakthrough discovery. At the end of his interview, the commander made his final declaration: "The *Stability Party* intended to kill the head of the mayor's office in order to take down the *Independence Party*."

At four p.m., I was officially released. Before I left the commander's office, he dismissed everyone else from the room. Then, he turned to me and said in a low, deliberate voice, "For confidential reasons, you are not allowed to deny this story. If you do, your life will be in danger."

I met his gaze and replied, "Don't worry. I'm a good and obedient boy."

He smiled, patted me on the shoulder, and let me go. I stepped outside, climbed into a waiting car, and they drove me home.

Chapter 7

It had been a while since my animal instinct had failed me. I wondered if something had changed inside me— if I had entered a new state of being. Countless things had happened to me, yet I no longer felt them as I once did. That terrified me. One of those events was my sister's husband's accident, his imprisonment, and his execution. But when I saw that all the misfortune had fallen solely upon him—that his death had ended the suffering—I told myself that my instincts had remained calm because no danger had come to me, my mother, or my sister. Another reason was Lucky Brother. Not only had he never left the family, but he had always been serene. Lucky Brother was just like our victim. As soon as he went away, bad things would suddenly happen to us. But if that lucky man sat with us—even just to eat fruit or dinner—everyone breathed easier, assured that our situation was safe and sound.

***

The driver, sent by the mayor to take me home, pulled up in front of the house and dropped me off. Then, without a word, he hit the gas and sped away. I had no idea why he was in such a hurry. There was no danger threatening him. Maybe he didn't want to face my mother and sister in person. Or perhaps he believed what he had heard—that they were kidnappers. Either way, I didn't dare enter the house, either. I had no idea what to say to my sister and mother. I couldn't reveal the truth, but if I didn't go inside, I had nowhere else to stay. Even though the mayor had warned me that the house was no longer safe or suitable for me, he had made no real effort to help. His only act of kindness was sending a car—with a timid driver—to take me home, sparing me the taxi fare. Had he not been embarrassed, he might have hand-delivered me to my mother in front of police headquarters.

I stood in front of the door for half an hour. By then, I worried that I might attract attention or cause controversy. So, with no choice left, I rang the doorbell. It took a while before someone finally opened the door. A fat, middle-aged woman stood there. For a moment, I thought I had rung the wrong doorbell. But then, I caught a glimpse of our yard. The woman stared at me, surprised. I was about to ask her something when— Lucky Brother appeared from the cellar. The moment he saw me, he shouted for mother and sister. The middle-aged woman, startled by his voice, stepped aside. I stepped inside, trembling with fear.

In the middle of the yard, I was greeted—With a hard kick to the ass from my sister. And a resounding slap from my mother. Well, that was no surprise. Given everything that had happened, I had expected worse. I didn't waste time—I darted to my room immediately. My mother and sister stormed in after me. My mother grabbed me by the collar and called me a bastard. My sister spat, "You're a good-for-nothing. You betrayed this family." I tried to keep my voice steady. "Lucky Brother should be here too. I need to explain everything." But my mother snapped, "What do you want with him? Spit it out, you useless, idle fool."

I refused to say anything until Lucky Brother came in. But the lucky madman stood motionless, making no effort to approach. Finally, my sister grabbed his hand and dragged him into the room.

I closed the door, sat down, and told them everything— from A to Z. My final words were the warning from the police commander. Of course, I twisted the truth a little. I tricked them—made it seem like the commander had included them in his warning, even though he had only spoken about me. The moment I finished speaking, their faces turned as white as a sheet. Only Lucky Brother remained unmoved, his relaxed posture making it clear that he wasn't fooled. My mother and sister had already planned to expose the truth with the help of *Stability Party* newspapers, but now, they hesitated—Because they were afraid for their own lives. If it had only been my life at risk, they wouldn't have thought twice about throwing me under the bus. They had easily accepted my sister's husband's death. Why would my fate be any different? But this time was different. This time, they were afraid for themselves. And for once, I had been clever enough to maneuver the situation so they wouldn't dare to plot against me. At least, that's what I hoped. I wasn't entirely sure. But seeing their nervous expressions—their anxiety—gave me some reassurance. Still, the only thing that truly calmed me was Lucky Brother. He lay carefree on the couch, his eyes drifting shut, completely ignoring us. At that moment, I knew—Nothing was going to happen to me.

After a long discussion about my disappearance, its consequences, and my sister's frustrated attempts to make sense of it all, the first thing I said was: "I'm hungry." My mother sighed. "We don't have any pots," she said. During the many protests—both for and against the parties—the pots had been punctured. They hadn't had a chance to buy new ones yet. As soon as she finished speaking, something shocking happened. Lucky Brother spoke. For the first and last time, he said something political. He opened his eyes, yawned loudly, and muttered: "Drat the *Independence Party*! They ruined our pots." And that was it. That was the moment I lost faith in the *Independence Party* completely.

My mother sent the middle-aged woman to buy food for me from a restaurant. I turned to Lucky Brother, who had witnessed everything, yet remained calm and carefree, and asked, "Who is this woman?"

Without rushing, he replied, "She's our housekeeper." His eyes sparkled with amusement.

***

My mother and sister didn't wait for the housekeeper to return. As soon as I finished speaking, they rushed out of the house—not bothering to tell me where they were going. But I knew. They were headed to the *Stability Party* Caucus to report everything they had just heard. Otherwise, they wouldn't have left at that speed, in the middle of the night. I didn't care about their plans. What mattered was the only true warning system I had—Lucky Brother. And right now, my adversity detector sat directly in front of me. His movements were slow, his hands still, as if they were about to stop working altogether. Nothing was going to happen tonight.

The housekeeper returned with food. I ate at ease, with appetite. Then, after all those troubled days, I lay down on my bed. And for the first time in a long time—I slept.

That night, I didn't even notice when they returned home. I had fallen asleep instantly and didn't wake up until late the next morning, when the sunlight had filled the entire house. I got up and went to the living room. My mother and sister were gone. It seemed that both of them had left early in the morning. The only person I saw was Lucky Brother, sitting in front of the TV, watching a Walt Disney cartoon. The housekeeper was nowhere to be seen either. I turned to Lucky Brother and asked, "Has she gone with them?"

He laughed and replied, "Fortunately, the housekeeper has nothing to do with the party."

At that moment, the housekeeper walked in. I handed her some money and sent her to buy all the morning newspapers for me. She left and returned a few minutes later. I took the newspapers and followed her into the kitchen. She placed my breakfast on the table. As I ate— slowly—I read through the papers.

What a famous person I had become!

Several newspapers had printed my large photo on the front page, with detailed accounts of the fear and suffering I had endured during my ten days in captivity. They had even published stories about my friendship with my sister's husband—From childhood up until the day of his arrest. One article claimed that my sister had exploited that friendship, using it to pressure him into marrying her. Another piece focused on my conscience and guilt—It described how I was tormented by the idea that I had unknowingly caused my sister and her husband to meet.

But the most interesting part? Not a single journalist had mentioned my sister or my mother in connection to my abduction. Instead, they only referred to "unknown kidnappers"—Mysterious individuals who had supposedly tried to defame the *Independence Party*. Some articles even speculated that the kidnappers might have been enemies of the mayor.

***

I read all the newspapers. Lucky Brother watched every TV program. The housekeeper cooked for all of us. Everything was ready—Except Mother and Sister were nowhere to be seen. Eventually, the three of us sat in the middle of the living room. Lucky Brother and the housekeeper played Ludo. I was bored out of my mind. I pressed the power button on the TV, which Lucky Brother had turned off. But after flipping through channels, I realized the programs were even more boring than before. The first channel had a cooking show. The second channel aired a roundtable discussion. The third channel talked about the Dutch experience with waste management. The fourth channel covered a landslide in Equatorial Guinea. The fifth channel featured American scientists debating the Titanic sinking. I kept hopping channels. The second channel's discussion ended, and the announcer declared that the next segment would focus on native trees of Colombian forests. I turned off the TV.

I stood up and walked to the window, glancing out at the courtyard. A little later, Mother and Sister finally arrived. As soon as Mother stepped inside, she winked at me—a silent command to follow her to her room. I went in immediately. She closed the door behind us. Then, she sat on the sofa and gestured for me to sit across from her. I obeyed. She took a deep breath and said, "Listen carefully, because I won't repeat this."

Then, she fell silent. I thought, for a moment, that she had changed her mind. But after a pause, she spoke again, her voice tired: "You are not allowed to go out for a while." "You are not allowed to speak to any journalists." "You should not, under any circumstances, stand in front of their cameras."

I was furious and snapped, "First of all, I didn't give an interview that day. Not a single word in my voice was broadcast. The police commander made everything up himself." "Secondly, I refuse to follow your orders. I was a prisoner of the *Independence Party* for ten days, and now you expect me to be a prisoner of the *Stability Party*?" "Enough. I'm writing a letter to all the newspapers and putting an end to this nonsense."

My mother's face darkened with anger. "You are not going to do that," she snapped.

At that moment, my sister entered the room. She could tell at a glance that Mother was on the verge of losing her temper because I refused to back down. For a brief moment, the thought crossed my mind—What if I just left? What if I walked out and stood on my own two feet?

But before I could dwell on it, my sister silently gestured for Mother to leave the room. Without a word, Mother obeyed. My sister sat down and told me about the long discussions she and Mother had been involved in—both the previous night and that morning.

"You aren't a prisoner," she said. "You just need to stay home during the day. But at night, we can go out together."

I scoffed. "I have no intention of stepping outside at night. Ten nights of that was more than enough."

She rolled her eyes. "Don't be ridiculous. You wouldn't be going out with strangers. Mom and I will be with you. Besides, you'll be at home during the day, not locked up in some hotel where you don't even understand how things work."

I exhaled sharply. "I'm tired of this life. Who am I supposed to tell that to?"

She sighed. "Fine. But why are you yelling? Forget about writing that letter."

I narrowed my eyes. "Why?"

She hesitated, then leaned in slightly.

"I shouldn't be saying this, but since you're so stubborn, I might as well tell you—to put your mind at ease."

"Right now, negotiations are happening between the *Independence* and *Stability Party* factions. They're likely to form an alliance soon."

"But," she added, "there are factions within both parties that oppose this coalition—"

"The same factions that kidnapped you and killed my husband."

I studied her face.

"Are you part of those opposing factions?"

She exhaled slowly.

"I was—until last night."

"But now, the situation has changed. Last night, I realized it's better to cooperate with those who support the coalition."

I crossed my arms.

"And what does any of this have to do with me?"

She smirked slightly.

"For starters, you're not going back to the mayor's office anymore."

"Because we have a better job for you."

I laughed bitterly.

"I'm not worried about work. But I am worried about being trapped at home all day, watching Lucky Brother and the housekeeper play Ludo."

My sister laughed.

"What, have you already gotten jealous?"

I scoffed.

"This isn't jealousy. What kind of job are you talking about? Don't I have my own life?"

She gave me a knowing look.

"Of course you have your own life. And it's about to change for the better."

"In a few days, you will be in charge of the headquarters of my late husband's companies. Everything will be yours."

I stared at her.

"So, you're saying I'll be the successor of deceased Othello?"

Her expression darkened.

"You never learn, do you?" she snapped. "Once something gets in your head, it never comes out."

I smirked.

"Am I wrong? I will be the successor of Othello."

Her anger flared.

"Why don't you shut up and stop calling him Othello?"

Chapter 8

Then, something unexpected happened—something that changed everything. Mother got married. I had been so engrossed in work that I hadn't even noticed what was happening with her and my sister. For a long time, I had forgotten about the parties. My days were filled with company tasks, and I barely left the headquarters from morning to evening. Even my meetings were held in the conference room of my office, where people came to me. Still, as usual, I would glance at the calendar every day, keeping track of the beginning and end of the weeks of happiness and sorrow. At night, I would go to a restaurant or a café, staying there until I got bored. The police never stopped me on my way to or from the café. Perhaps that was why I had never bothered to attend my mother and sister's political gatherings. I remained completely unaware of everything.

It was Lucky Brother who informed me about Mother's marriage. He was absolutely thrilled. "Why are you so happy?" I asked, raising an eyebrow. "What's in it for you?"

He looked at me, maintaining his usual calm expression, and said, "Mom says my dad is coming home."

***

Mother's wedding party was held at the Industrial Club. My sister, Lucky Brother, my nephew, and I all went together. Mother had left home early in the morning and was set to arrive at the club later with her close friends. When we arrived, the groom was already there. But Mother had not yet arrived.

The groom was a dignified man. Tall, with thick, solid gray hair. I had never heard anything about him before. No one had mentioned his name. But from his appearance alone, I could tell—He was a fat cat. The venue he had chosen for the wedding, the guests surrounding him—For a brief moment, my heart swelled with pride. Then, just as quickly, I remembered Father. This man—this new husband of Mother's— He was a far cry from the man who had raised us. Finally, Mother had corrected the mistake she made in her youth. But how late it was. I thought, If only she hadn't made that mistake when she was young... Or worse—if only she hadn't made an even bigger mistake afterward. Then, maybe—just maybe— We wouldn't have had to endure everything that followed. Maybe we wouldn't have been forced into this chaotic life. Maybe we wouldn't have had to be born into madness just to find happiness.

I greeted the groom briefly. I wished the mayor had been at the party—Just so he could see how far I had come. So he would know that even after leaving his office, I had not been humiliated. I was now the manager of my sister's companies. And our new stepfather? A fat cat. Meanwhile, Lucky Brother showed no regard for the solemnity of the party. He clung to the groom like a leech. Annoyed, my sister gave me a silent signal. I took him aside and asked one of my employees to take him outside and play with him in the courtyard.

The party didn't last long. Neither Mother nor her new husband had the stamina for a long event— They were no spring chickens. Ladies had gathered around Mother, surrounding her so completely that I could barely get close enough to congratulate her. She seemed surprised by my hurried approach. Though she didn't say anything, I could see it in her expression. Still, I kept it brief. "Congratulations. I should have congratulated you earlier."

Mother simply smiled in response.

That night, after the guests had left, I was able to talk to my stepfather for about half an hour—until my mother arrived, and they both got into their car and drove off to his house.

He seemed like a kind man. From what he and those around him had said, I gathered that he was a friend of the major shareholders of both the *Independence* and *Stability* Parties. There wasn't much time for a deeper conversation that night. My sister, brother, and nephew walked Mother and her new husband to the door, watching as they got into their car. Lucky Brother tried to go along with them, but I clasped his hand and stopped him.

On our way back home, I turned to my sister and said, "No one in our family—or even among our relatives—has ever been as wise as Mother." My sister immediately tensed. She assumed I was insulting her. Her expression darkened, and she remained silent the entire ride home. When we arrived, she sulked off to her room and didn't come out until morning.

Around noon, Mother called. I congratulated her again—But this time, I truly spoke my mind. "I think this blessed marriage won't just solve our family's problems," I told her, "but also many of the country's problems. Above all..." I paused for dramatic effect. "Our pots won't be punctured anymore."

Mother burst into laughter. At the sound of her amusement, Sister suddenly emerged from her room and stretched out her hand to grab the phone. I gestured that I wasn't done yet—But I waited for Mother's laughter to die down before continuing. "Of course," I added, "before you, Sister was the only one in the family who ever used her intellect and acted wisely. "But, Mother... You scored the winning goal in the nick of time." "I think history itself has pushed you forward to solve the country's problems."

Mother thought I was making fun of her. Sister thought the same—Because she hit me in the chest with her palm and snatched the phone from my hand. Even though I had nothing else to say, I looked at her and said, "I'm not making fun of anyone. "Maybe there's no need for a speech, but I truly believe Mother's marriage is blessed."

Mother's life with her new husband was peaceful and harmonious—A far cry from the life she had lived with my father. We lived apart for only one month. But in truth, it was Mother who had separated from us— She had been the one to move out and settle into her husband's house. Despite that, we were never out of touch. She called us several times a day and came to visit us every other day. She had become remarkably kind to us. Though I rarely saw her, she often took Lucky Brother out, driving around the city together. Many times, I noticed that when he returned home with Mother, he no longer resembled the calm, peaceful boy he once was. Instead, he would raise a ruckus—his energy spreading to everyone in the house. But I was happy. Everything at home was calm. Everything was harmonious. And, for the first time in a long time, I could focus on my work—Without anxiety. Without concern.

We were just getting used to our new life when something important happened—Something we had been anticipating ever since the night of Mother's wedding. Of course, I never thought it would happen so soon. It was Mother herself who called and informed Sister— The *Independence Party* had officially formed a coalition with the *Stability Party*. I assumed this new alliance would bring even more peace to our home. What we didn't expect was how significant this coalition would be for our lives. With the new political order, Mother's husband was appointed Minister of Industries. At the same time, our family's status rose dramatically. The Minister himself called me and asked me to meet him immediately. I ended a meeting I had just begun and went straight to his office. I congratulated him on his appointment. He hugged me and kissed me on both cheeks, then led me into the meeting room. A staff member brought me coffee, but the Minister apologized, explaining that he couldn't spend much time with me.

"I've wanted us all to live together from the very beginning," he admitted.

I hesitated before answering.

"It's better not to intrude," I said.

"You and Mother should be comfortable together."

But he shook his head.

"No, your presence won't disturb us," he insisted.

"My house is huge—even if a hundred people lived in it, no one would feel crowded."

And so, we vacated our old home, rented it out, and moved our belongings to my stepfather's house. It was, as he had claimed, a massive estate on the outskirts of the city. Lucky Brother was ecstatic— Finally, he had a place big enough to flaunt himself. For the first time, he didn't feel trapped in a cage. Mother's husband was kind to him, giving him more freedom than he had ever known. Even the housekeeper moved with us—She became Lucky Brother's personal servant, while my stepfather's existing staff worked harder to manage the large household.

***

Not only did Mother play a leading role in the Women's Organization of the *Stability Party*, but she had also become the most influential figure in the Women's Organization of the entire country. I often warned her to take better care of her health. "At your age, you should slow down a little," I advised. "Spend more time with your husband—look after him." But Mother paid no attention to my words.

Sister also lived freely, unconcerned with her duties as a widow and mother. With Othello gone, we had all forgotten him. The only reminder of his existence was my nephew's last name. Fortunately, the boy looked nothing like Othello—And we only called him by his first name. His last name was never mentioned except for official documents. I managed all the companies on my own, only handing financial statements to Sister occasionally. She glanced at them carelessly, uninterested. She had no patience for business matters. She was a wanderer—Even worse than Lucky Brother, because he at least had to confine his antics to the estate. But Sister? She had found a circus as wide as the world.

***

We all assumed that our world had changed permanently. That we would never have to think about the past again. But for some reason, the past kept creeping into my mind. I began to remember Father. I recalled the stories he used to tell me about Mother— Stories I had completely forgotten for years. Suddenly, those memories returned with all their details. And I couldn't shake the feeling that they were a warning— A bad omen. My animal instinct stirred again. It shook me from the inside. Moment by moment, my concern grew. That internal trembling left me no doubt— These happy days were temporary. A disaster was coming. But what would happen? I started watching everyone carefully. My suspicions fell most heavily on Sister. She had hired a nanny to care for her son—Living her life freely, unburdened by any responsibilities. No matter how hard I tried to talk to her properly, I never succeeded—She was rarely home. I never put the calendar away. I checked it constantly. And whenever a special ceremony was approaching, I warned everyone to be careful. But Mother's husband would always laugh and say, "The police officer foolish enough to approach us would be sent somewhere to beg for mercy." "Nothing threatens us. You just take care of yourself."

After my stepfather's remarks, Sister leaned in and whispered in my ear, "Did you hear that? Nobody's in danger—except you. Honestly, you should go get yourself checked out. You're losing your mind."

But I didn't give up. I waited for the right time— A time when Mother's husband was not at home. And then, I spoke up to Mother and Sister. "I think there's a real danger threatening us," I warned. They both laughed at me. They mocked me. Sister went so far as to say, "It's the words that come out of your mouth that bring misfortune on this family. "Just like the hoo-hoo of an owl." From that day on, they all called me Owl.

***

The misfortune soon revealed itself. It came in the form of death. Mother's husband was killed. He had been on his way home from the ministry when his car plunged off a bridge into the river. Both he and his driver were killed instantly. When the police called, Mother and Sister were not at home. So, I went to the scene of the accident alone. There, I watched as officers used a crane to pull the car from the water. I stood by the bridge railing, observing silently. The police commander approached me, pointed at a large trailer parked near the bridge, and said, "Apparently, that trailer caused the accident." "The driver claims he lost control due to the heavy rain and swerved into the minister's car." "The minister's driver tried to pull over to avoid a collision— but the corroded bridge railing gave way, sending them into the river."

It took an hour to retrieve the car. The body of Mother's husband was covered in mud. They quickly removed him from the wreckage and transported him to the forensic pathology department by ambulance. I followed behind. By the time the corpse was being prepared for examination, Mother and Sister had arrived. I didn't know who had informed them. Mother was weeping. Sister looked stunned—motionless. I pulled them aside and warned them firmly: "You cannot give interviews. Say nothing until you know for sure what happened."

The whole thing looked like a conspiracy. I wasn't worried about Mother's husband. He had lived his life. He had died painlessly. But what concerned me deeply was the fragility of the coalition between the

Independence and *Stability* Parties. If it collapsed, the war between them would start all over again. The fear consumed me. I was so on edge that I couldn't even focus on my work. I pleaded with Sister for help. She handed me Othello's old card and said, "Go to Shell Café and forget everything." So, that became my routine. Every night, I escaped to Shell Café, staying there until morning. Then, I'd return home, sleep until the afternoon, and repeat the cycle. Because of this, I saw Mother and Sister less and less. It was better that way. It meant fewer arguments. Fewer accusations. Honestly, I stopped caring about them altogether. I didn't know where they went. I only knew they were never home.

***

I hadn't heard from the Mayor in a long time. And, to be honest, it had never even crossed my mind to ask about him. Even though I knew he was no longer the mayor, to me, he would always be the mayor. Of course, I assumed I would eventually see him at Shell Café. But even if he was there, the place was so discreet and controlled that we might never run into each other. One night, as I sat at my usual table, the café attendant slipped a note onto my table. I had been there less than thirty minutes. I stood up immediately and left. A car was waiting for me outside. The café manager stood next to it. I turned to him and said, "I already have a car. Just tell me where I'm supposed to go."

The manager stepped closer and said, "Your car stays here. You'll be back soon."

I didn't know where they were taking me. But I knew I was going to meet the Mayor. I surrendered myself to fate. But as soon as I saw the tall silhouette of the Shell Hotel in the distance— My arms and legs went numb with fear. The fifteenth floor. That damn room. That was the only thing I was afraid of. I wanted to ask the driver where we were going. But then I remembered: Drivers don't know anything. They just follow orders. Before I could think of what to do, the car slid down into the parking lot entrance.

At the elevator doors, it wasn't the hotel manager who greeted me. Instead, a smartly dressed young man opened the car door. I rushed into the elevator. But something was off. The elevator barely moved. It stopped almost immediately. I was expecting the fifteenth floor. Instead, we arrived at the first. The doors opened, and I was led into a room. Inside, waiting for me—Was the former mayor.

After a brief greeting, the mayor stated that the coalition between the two parties had come to an end and warned me to be cautious about my mother's and sister's activities. He then added that they had received reliable information indicating that the *Stability Party* intended to create chaos. The coalition with the *Independence Party* had not yielded favorable results for them, and many of their supporters had shifted allegiance to the *Independence Party*.

He spoke at length that night, spinning a cock-and-bull story. I gazed out the window, barely listening to what he was saying. When he finally dismissed me, the only thing I could recall was that I was expected to become a party spy.

I accepted the mission willingly—but not out of loyalty to the *Independence Party*. No, my real motivation was to uncover the truth about my mother and sister, as they had not been staying at home for some time. My sister had even gone weeks without seeing her son. Of course, I trusted my mother. That does not mean I distrusted my sister, but she had demonstrated her vigilance before—most notably in the case of Othello's execution. As for my mother, she had come to her senses after marrying my stepfather.

As soon as I returned from the Shell Café, I did not sleep. Instead, I waited for my mother and sister to wake up. When they did, I told them that I intended to join the *Stability Party*. In their presence, I mailed my *Independence Party* membership card to the party's headquarters. My mother and sister were pleased with my decision.

The *Stability Party* issued me a membership card almost immediately. On my first day as a member, I informed the mayor that my mother and sister had been invited to a secret meeting where the party would decide the fate of the coalition.

***

The chaos erupted soon after. First, the newspapers got involved. Overnight, our once-quiet home—the house left to us by my mother's late husband—was transformed into a storage room for newspapers, much like that haunted room atop the Shell Hotel. Every day, the servants delivered stacks of newspapers, and my mother and sister, with utmost seriousness, cut out articles related to the *Stability* and *Independence* Parties, filing them into separate folders.

The newspapers of both parties launched relentless attacks, hurling insults and accusations without restraint. Every night, I asked my mother for updates on the *Stability Party*'s affairs. As always, my sister spoke little. I suspected she still did not trust me.

But that was only part of the issue. The deeper truth was that she was a woman of action.

The *Independence Party* terminated the coalition cabinet and formed a weak government with the support of two small parties, Justice and Progress. This outcome was predictable and surprised no one. However, what no one expected was the sudden reopening of the case regarding the late Othello's execution. The newspapers affiliated with the *Independence Party* brought the issue to light the day after the new cabinet was formed.

Suddenly, my family found itself bombarded with insults and various accusations. Almost every newspaper dedicated at least one column to our family history in each issue. Even I was not spared from the accusations. Of course, I was not troubled by them at all. In fact, I was even relieved, as they served as a convenient distraction, concealing my role as a spy and, most importantly, gaining my sister's trust. At first, I did not fear the accusations, but soon, the situation escalated. My sister came under suspicion, and fear took hold of me. Yet, at the time, I did not fully understand why I was so unsettled. My instincts remained calm, reassuring me that there was no real danger. My only concern was that my sister might make a reckless move in response to the accusations.

Then, unexpectedly, something even more significant occurred, overshadowing the controversy surrounding Othello's execution. In the midst of the uproar, the ministers of the *Stability Party* in the coalition government were arrested. The official newspapers reported that they were the masterminds behind years of conspiracies.

Despite this shift in focus, my mother and sister still feared that my sister might be summoned to court due to the reopening of Othello's case. Our house was a constant flurry of activity, with multiple telephone lines ringing day and night. However, I assured my sister that those phone calls were pointless and that she had nothing to worry about. My instincts told me everything would be fine. Upon hearing my words, my sister looked at my mother in astonishment and said, "Mom! The world has truly turned upside down. The owl brings good news."

***

The *Independence Party* celebrated its victory on a national scale. The entire country was swept up in exhilaration, but unlike everyone else, our family was in mourning. For quite some time, my sister had been extremely cautious whenever she left the house. She often returned home early, preferring the safety of our residence—especially since it was located in the countryside. Not all of us were upset, though. My "lucky" brother, for instance, was so pleased that he no longer wanted to leave the house at all.

Despite our grief, we decided to participate in the national celebrations. My sister, however, opposed the idea from the start, insisting that she would stay home. She did not want to hear the cheers and shouts of the people.

Since my stepfather's house was in the countryside, attending the celebrations regularly was inconvenient. Therefore, we decided to go to our former home—my father's house—which had been vacant for several months. On the morning of the celebration, my lucky brother, my mother, and I quickly got into the car. Before leaving, I urged my sister to join us, but she merely clasped her son's hand and retreated to her room in anger.

The housekeepers and servants had already gone ahead by car to prepare everything. The city was unrecognizable compared to how it had looked just days before. Everywhere we turned, we saw the Nosrat Arches and large and small vases filled with flowers. We marveled at how they had managed to gather so many flowers in just a week, from the announcement of the celebration to its actual commencement.

My mother had instructed the servants to buy baskets of flowers, which they had placed on the balcony. However, there was still some empty space. To fill the gaps, she ordered them to bring in fresh geraniums from the yard. Finally, we placed a large tape recorder behind the vases to play cheerful music.

When the celebration began, the leaders of the *Independence Party* paraded through the streets in sunroof cars. They did not pass all at once. One car would drive by, then another would arrive half an hour later, and we would throw flowers at them from the balcony. This continued until the new mayor, who was also a member of the *Independence Party*, appeared from the front street.

Everyone was happily tossing flower branches, and most of them came from our house. Following my mother's orders, the servants and housekeepers threw flowers so persistently that the mayor took notice and stopped beneath our balcony. He looked up and recognized us. Then, in an attempt to taunt us, he raised two fingers of his right hand. I turned around and glanced at my mother. Her posture was odd—on the one hand, she wanted to appear indifferent to his victory, yet on the other, she was visibly frowning.

The mayor remained still, holding up his fingers. I did not understand his gesture. Perhaps he was trying to say, "One in the eye for you—we have won."

We carried on, throwing flowers until our baskets were empty. Not knowing what to do next, we hesitated— until suddenly, my lucky brother grabbed a large vase filled with geraniums and hurled it from the balcony. None of us saw it coming, and neither did the unfortunate mayor. The vase landed squarely on his head.

Chaos erupted instantly. The music stopped, replaced by screams and shouts from every direction. It was as if the crowd had been waiting for such an incident—ready to yell in place of the cassette recorder.

Within moments, they arrested me, my mother, and my lucky brother. At the police station, we soon realized that the servants and housekeepers had also been detained. Shortly after, my sister and her son arrived. She informed us that, within less than an hour, our house had been looted—despite being on the outskirts of the city. The officers and supporters of the *Independence Party* had taken everything.

Then, without explanation, some officers came and took my brother away.

I no longer doubted the fallacy of my mother's predictions. In the end, he had become an unfortunate soul. My sister and I were on high alert—not only for his sake but for our own survival. Yet my mother remained eerily composed, as if nothing had happened.

At the police station, I remarked sarcastically, "So this was the fate of our insane brother's happiness."

My mother shot me a hateful glare and said, "Make sure he doesn't even get a paper cut."

Three days later, they allowed us to see my lucky brother for the first time. His head and face were covered in blood, and he could barely speak. The meeting lasted only a few moments—they simply showed him to us and then took him away again.

***

They interrogated us day and night for a week. By the end of it, I felt brain-dead. My body had been numb since the first day, battered by relentless beatings. My mother and sister were held in separate prisons, and the only news I received was that my sister's son was safe. Out of respect for the late Othello, the leaders of the *Independence Party* had ensured that his son remained unaware of his mother's terrible situation.

My beatings had ended after the first day of imprisonment. After that, they took me from one place to another, constantly moving me. At first, I did not mind—I even enjoyed it. But when they overdid it, my patience wore thin. If they had kept it within limits, I would have tolerated it. I had expected the leaders of the *Independence Party* to intervene on my behalf—at least for my sake—but no matter how long I waited, there was no sign of them. I grew angry at their indifference and decided that, at the right time, I would make them pay for their disregard and disrespect.

At the beginning of the week, they took me to see my insane brother. My mother was no longer there to insist that he would not even get a paper cut. My task was to extract the name of the person who had provoked him into his actions. I knew he was not one of those people, but I had no choice—I had to cooperate. If I refused, not only would my brother's situation worsen, but I would also find myself in unknown and dire consequences.

My brother was far from cautious. He was utterly lost in confusion, unable even to wail. No matter how much I tried to provoke him, he remained silent. His lips were sealed. The officers quickly realized that he was not pretending—he genuinely lacked the ability to speak properly. He had struggled to articulate words even before this incident. Now, he was completely at a loss for words.

***

I had just returned from my meeting with my brother. The officers had thrown me back into my cell when, moments later, the door swung open again. I assumed they had come to torment me once more, but to my surprise, a new officer entered and gently pulled me to my feet. He led me out of the cell with unexpected kindness. I thought to myself, What a wonderful and noble man! At least with him, I would have a few moments of peace. However, I could not understand why he was in such a hurry. Couldn't he slow down so that we'd arrive later—wherever it was he was taking me? Before I could dwell on it further, we arrived at the prison chief's office. As we stepped inside, the chief himself stood up and walked toward me. I was astonished—he seemed even kinder than his officer. He took my hand and gently guided me to sit on the couch beside him. He was visibly flustered. Pacing back and forth, he seemed unable to compose himself. I wondered what could have happened to cause such a dramatic shift in their behavior toward me. I wanted to tell him to sit down at his desk and say something, but I reminded myself that I was still a prisoner. Then, I glanced down at my hands. They were free. Why hadn't they put handcuffs on me, as they always did when I left my cell?

The officer, looking uncertain, finally spoke: "Would you like something to eat? We can prepare anything you want as soon as possible."

Curious to test them, I said quietly, "A can of Pepsi-Cola."

The officer immediately stood up and rushed toward me. Instinctively, I leaned back on the sofa, wary of his sudden movement. But he stopped just short, standing near me as though I were the boss. Then, in a voice full of respect, he asked:

"Would it be a problem if it's Coca-Cola instead?"

I replied, "No. But make sure it's cold. Bring one from the fridge."

He made a phone call, and in the blink of an eye, another officer arrived with a tray carrying a red can of Coca-Cola. The first officer took the tray from him and bowed in front of me. I looked at him, then picked up the can— it was cold. The officer himself opened it, and I drank every last drop with peace of mind. When I was finished, the officer respectfully took the empty can from my hand and passed it to the second officer to dispose of.

Half an hour later, they brought in my mother and sister. Their appearance made it clear that they had not fared any better than I had during that week. As always, my sister was angry and confused, while my mother remained calm and composed.

I asked my sister what had happened, but neither she nor my mother knew. I suggested that our unfortunate brother might have revealed everything. My sister scoffed, "Whatever happens to him serves him right." But my mother, with the same unwavering calmness, said, "You'd better think of yourself. I've said a hundred times—he won't even get a paper cut."

I laughed. "Perhaps there is no longer a body."

My mother grinned and turned her back to me.

When the reporters arrived, we finally understood what had happened. On the last day of the week, the newspapers affiliated with the *Stability Party* had published espionage documents exposing the mayor— who was aligned with the *Independence Party* and still in a coma.

Suddenly, our unfortunate brother's status changed overnight. Every newspaper featured his full-face photo on the front page, branding him a national hero. The news sent shockwaves through the country, dominating the headlines. Yet, amidst the uproar, my mother remained indifferent to it all. She simply requested that we be taken to visit our brother as soon as possible.

They promptly arranged a car, and we were taken to the central prison.

We found my lucky brother in the infirmary, where a team of doctors was working tirelessly to remove the scars from his beatings. It was then that I stared into my mother's eyes. She had never made predictions about anyone—except for my brother. But how had her prophecy come true?

Despite our astonishment, my brother did not complain. He had surrendered himself entirely to the doctors, lying there with his usual indifference, unmoved by either pain or the news of his sudden rise to fame.

That night, we were all released from prison. They placed us in a car and drove us home with utmost respect. But home—if it could still be called that—was now a shanty. The ransacking had left it in ruins. They had released the servants and housekeepers before setting us free. My mother sent them out to buy supplies for our rest and recovery. Then, without delay, she wrote a long, detailed list of all the damages and sent it to the court, formally requesting that the *Independence Party* be held accountable for compensation.

I never returned to the Shell Café—I could no longer bear to associate with the *Independence Party*. The thought of it embarrassed me. Despite my unwavering support for them, despite enduring brutal beatings and persecution until the very last day, they had done nothing to help me. Meanwhile, the *Stability Party* had gone to great lengths to save my mother and sister. Not only had they rescued them, but they had also secured my release and even assigned my lucky brother a high-ranking position.

This time, I was not deprived of my sister's kindness. When she realized I no longer went to the Shell Café, she handed me a permanent membership card for the Orchid Café.

***

The controversy surrounding the mayor's espionage scandal worsened day by day. In parliament, tensions escalated as members turned against each other until, finally, the parliament was dissolved, forcing early elections. No one played a greater role in shaping the future of the government than lucky brother. The *Stability Party* provided him with a private plane, a helicopter, and a car to take him to different cities. Everywhere he went, people welcomed him with enthusiasm. Standing before the crowds, he uttered just one sentence:

"I killed the spy."

Thanks to lucky brother, I stayed completely uninvolved. During the day, I managed my sister's businesses, and at night, I spent my time at the Orchid Café, lingering there until I grew bored. This routine allowed me to steer clear of their political schemes. But behind the scenes, my mother and sister controlled lucky brother from the shadows. He was at the center of the storm, while those two, armed with two phone lines, spent their days making calls or traveling in their cars. Even my sister's son was enlisted to assist them.

In an interview, my sister publicly declared her son a victim of the *Independence Party*, saying that if the leaders of that party had not deceived his father, he would have grown up under his father's protection.

The *Stability Party*'s victory in the elections was unprecedented in the country's history. And I couldn't help but wonder—if my mother, my sister, and most of all, lucky brother had not interfered, would such a monumental political shift have taken place?

When the newspapers published the election results, the names of the newly elected representatives appeared with the *Stability Party*'s emblem printed beside them—proof of their landslide victory.

Ultimately, thanks to that election—and more specifically, to lucky brother's historic decision to throw the geranium vase—our family secured an influential position.

With the formation of the new, powerful government led by the *Stability Party*, my mother was appointed Deputy Prime Minister for Women's Affairs.

The moment the news was announced on television, we all jumped up in joy, showering my mother with kisses. Yet, amid our celebrations, the true architect of our success remained seated on the sofa, watching us with his usual calm expression.

Without delay, my mother had her car prepared, and we headed to the *Stability Party* headquarters—to hold the real party there.

Chapter 9

The former mayor telephoned the company headquarters several times, but I ignored his messages. In my opinion, he was no longer important—just grasping at straws. He must have known it too, which was why he was careful not to call my home. But eventually, his patience ran out. Furious, he sent a message to my secretary: if I did not return his call, he would expose everything in an interview. So, I called him. He was livid. "You must come to the café tonight," he growled. "Otherwise, I'll put your ass in a sling."

That night, I went to the Shell Café. I had barely sat down when the waiter approached me. "A car is waiting for you outside," he said. I stepped outside, taking my time. I was about to break the law, so I wanted witnesses. Speaking loudly, I addressed the café's manager before turning to scan my surroundings. The dim lighting made it difficult to see, but I caught sight of two men near the manager, pointing at him in surprise. I did not recognize them. The manager suddenly grabbed my arm and led me toward the car. The driver had already opened the door. Without hesitation, the manager shoved me inside. On the way, I felt nauseous and told the driver to slow down. He ignored me.

Unlike the last time, the Shell Hotel's manager took me straight to the fifteenth floor—to that damn room. Maybe he wanted to scare me. If so, he succeeded. The moment I saw the door, my entire body trembled with fear. Then, he left me there. Alone. That was even worse. The mayor was toying with me, trying to crush me with anxiety before even entering the room. I knew his game, but there was nothing I could do. The memory of those ten horrible days I had once spent in this room haunted me, refusing to let me stay calm. Of course, my inner restlessness wasn't the kind that signaled impending doom. Yet fear still gripped my heart, making my body go numb. So when the mayor finally walked in, I was already on my knees.

The mayor didn't say much. He just wanted me to work for the *Independence Party* again—not as a member, but as an informant. He wanted me to tell him what was happening in our house. I refused. "I can't do that," I said. "My family already suspects me. They think my refusal to participate in the elections proves I support the *Independence Party*. They see me as the spy."

But the mayor wasn't born yesterday. Placing a firm hand on my shoulder, he said, "Don't play dumb. We're not fooled by your words. Drop the lies and listen carefully. If you don't keep me informed, I'll make your espionage story public. I'll publish some of the information you've already given us. You know exactly what will happen to you then."

He was right. If that story became public, I would be kicked out of my home without a second thought. So, I promised to cooperate. But I swore I wasn't in a position to give him any information at that moment. Just like before, I resumed my routine at the Shell Café, waiting for the right opportunity. The mayor had given me clear instructions: whenever I overheard anything from the members of the *Stability Party*, I was to report directly to him.

And I obeyed.

1996

Asemana Books is devoted to publishing diasporic,

underrepresented, and progressive literature on the Middle East.

asemanabooks.ca

ASEMANA
BOOKS